Gardiner had noticed her a few times—world-class legs, Panama hat, gaudy jewelry and all. Okay, he'd noticed her *a lot* of times.

She'd come in the day after he had. Twice already he had barely escaped being seated with her in the hotel's only dining room. It seemed the staff was committed by blood oath to pair up spares. But he'd paid for his right to be here, and no long-legged, nose-in-the-air female was going to make him hole up in his room! He wasn't afraid of her. He wasn't even *interested* in her!

He willed himself to concentrate on the exotic scenery, on the cold beer he was about to enjoy—on anything at all except for a certain pair of large dark eyes, a certain lean, seductive body with a great way of walking....

Dear Reader:

Welcome to Silhouette Desire! If you're a regular reader, you already know you're in for a treat. If this is your first Silhouette Desire, I predict you'll be hooked on romance, because these are sensuous, emotional love stories written by and for today's women—women just like *you!*

A Silhouette Desire can have many different moods and tones: some are humorous, others dramatic. But they *all* have a heroine you can identify with. She's busy, smart, and occasionally downright frazzled! She's always got something keeping her on the go: family, sometimes kids, maybe a job and there's that darned car that keeps breaking down! And of course, she's got that extra complication—the sexy, interesting man she's just met....

Speaking of sexy men, don't miss May's *Man of the Month* title, *Sweet on Jessie,* by Jackie Merritt. This man is just wonderful. Also, look for *Just Say Yes,* another terrific romance from the pen of Dixie Browning. Rounding out May are books by Lass Small, Rita Rainville, Cait London and Christine Rimmer. It's a great lineup, and naturally I hope you read them all.

So, until next month, happy reading!

Lucia Macro
Senior Editor

DIXIE BROWNING

JUST SAY YES

SILHOUETTE *Desire*®

Published by Silhouette Books New York

America's Publisher of Contemporary Romance

SILHOUETTE BOOKS
300 East 42nd St., New York, N.Y. 10017

JUST SAY YES

ISBN: 0-373-05637-0

First Silhouette Books printing May 1991

Printed in the U.S.A.

Books by Dixie Browning

Silhouette Romance

Unreasonable Summer #12
Tumbled Wall #38
Chance Tomorrow #53
Wren of Paradise #73
East of Today #93
Winter Blossom #113
Renegade Player #142
Island on the Hill #164
Logic of the Heart #172
Loving Rescue #191
A Secret Valentine #203
Practical Dreamer #221
Visible Heart #275
Journey to Quiet Waters #292
The Love Thing #305
First Things Last #323
Something for Herself #381
Reluctant Dreamer #460
A Matter of Timing #527
The Homing Instinct #747

Silhouette Books

Silhouette Christmas Stories 1987
"Henry the Ninth"

Silhouette Desire

Shadow of Yesterday #68
Image of Love #91
The Hawk and the Honey #111
Late Rising Moon #121
Stormwatch #169
The Tender Barbarian #188
Matchmaker's Moon #212
A Bird in Hand #234
In the Palm of Her Hand #264
A Winter Woman #324
There Once Was a Lover #337
Fate Takes a Holiday #403
Along Came Jones #427
Thin Ice #474
Beginner's Luck #517
Ships in the Night #541
Twice in a Blue Moon #588
Just Say Yes #637

Silhouette Special Edition

Finders Keepers #50
Reach Out to Cherish #110
Just Deserts #181
Time and Tide #205
By Any Other Name #228
The Security Man #314
Belonging #414

DIXIE BROWNING

has written over forty books for Silhouette since 1980. She is a charter member of the Romance Writers of America, and an award-winning author. A charismatic lecturer, Dixie has toured extensively for Silhouette Books, participating in "How to Write a Romance" workshops all over the country.

To Lou and Linda

One

It had been lust at first sight. Gardiner didn't like it. He didn't like *her*. But he'd noticed her a few times—world-class legs, Panama hat, gaudy jewelry and all. Okay, he'd noticed her a lot of times. It was hard to miss a woman who went around wearing little more than a shirt, a battered straw hat, and a piece of tin the size of a hubcap dangling from each ear. Even without those endless legs of hers, she had the kind of looks that wars had been fought over. And lost.

He figured she was probably a model. All gloss, no substance. Where Gardiner Gentry, professor of mathematics at a small but excellent college, was concerned, women of the most ordinary kind were an alien species. Beautiful specimens who stalked past him with their noses in the air had a way of stripping him down

to the naked needy soul, making him aware all over
again of what he'd come from.

He stared after her, shaking his head. After the fiasco with Georgia Riggs, you'd think he would've
learned something. No matter how far he'd risen from
his beginnings, a man didn't get dumped by a woman
half his age without suffering some self-doubt. This
trip, after all, was supposed to have been his honeymoon.

Gardiner had been headed for the stretch of beach
beyond the hotel property when he'd seen her. He preferred the rough weed-strewn coral, with its driftwood
snags and blowholes, to the freshly combed white sand
with its neat row of thatched-roofed lounge chairs and
its regiment of carefully lined trash cans.

He also preferred his own company to that of the
dozen or so muscle-bound jocks and scantily covered
females sporting about on the beach, their radios blar-
ing away in competition with the hotel's nonstop taped
music.

Panama Hat wasn't wearing a bikini. She was wearing a high-necked, long-sleeved pajama-top-looking-
thing that could drive a man wild wondering what was
under it. From his vantage point several yards behind
the row of beach chairs, all Gardiner could see was hat,
shirt and a couple of chunks of silver and turquoise.

And the legs, of course. By now, they were stretched
out in front of her, half in the sun, half in the shade. As
if she didn't give a damn in hell whether or not she got
an even tan.

During his brief affair with Georgia, Gardiner had
learned that getting an even tan rated right up there
with making it past the pearly gates. With a woman like

Panama Hat, he'd have thought it ranked a notch higher.

Shoving his book in his hip pocket, he switched his bottle of Mexican beer to his other hand and absently slapped at a mosquito. Time to move on. Time to start the tedious process of relaxing. It wasn't something he was good at—so far, he'd never found time to learn. But having bought the tickets, made the reservations and paid in advance, he was determined to salvage something out of this damned honeymoon-for-one.

What he deserved was a good solid kick in the butt, not a reward, for being such a fool. But it had been too late to switch things back, for he had already arranged to be away from his classes. And since he had the time coming to him, he'd decided to go through with the trip. The last thing he'd needed was to hang around town and run into Georgia or one of her friends. They were probably laughing themselves silly over the poor jerk who'd thought that when a woman said she loved everything about a man—he'd been stark naked and dripping wet at the time—it meant she was ready to marry him. A jerk who thought that when he suggested arranging his work load to get away for a couple of weeks in January, and she suggested somewhere warm and tropical, they were both talking honeymoon.

Okay, so he wasn't too old to learn from his mistakes. For six weeks he'd acted like a jackass over a bubble-brained cheerleader. At least he was getting a much-needed vacation out of it. On the other hand, he was beginning to wish he'd booked them into some place a little less couple-oriented. As a single, he stood out in stark relief.

So did Panama Hat. She'd come in the day after he had, and twice already he had barely escaped being seated with her in the hotel's only dining room. It seemed the staff was committed by blood oath to pairing up spares—even those who had developed an instant dislike for one another.

As a light breeze off the Caribbean tempered the brilliant winter sun, Gardiner Gentry felt a bit more of the tension he'd brought with him begin to ebb away. What the devil—women were everywhere. The trick was to learn to ignore them, to treat them as if they were genderless. Having grown up in an all-male household, worked in a male-dominated area until he'd joined the army, graduated from a largely male college and taken a position in an all-male school—one of the last of its kind in existence—he was about as comfortable around women as he was around boa constrictors.

It hadn't helped that he had stuttered until he was nearly twenty, and even now, in times of great stress, he had trouble getting his words out. Maybe that was why he'd gone into the field of mathematics. Math was self-explanatory. It was stress-free. At least it had always seemed so to him.

Gardiner willed himself now to concentrate on the exotic scenery, on the cold beer he was about to enjoy—on anything at all except a certain pair of large dark eyes, a certain lean seductive body, with a great way of walking that set up a whole system of fascinating harmonic reactions.

Not to mention a low sexy chuckle that gave rise to a totally inappropriate physical response whenever he happened to hear it.

Armed with his liquid refreshment and the latest best-selling mystery, he stalked on past the row of palapa-shaded lounges toward the wild unkempt spit of a coral beach that jutted into the Caribbean. He'd paid for his right to be here. Dammit, paid double! No long-legged nose-in-the-air female was going to make him hole up in his room under a creaking ceiling fan! He wasn't afraid of her. He wasn't even *interested* in her!

Daisy stood it as long as she could. Sweating under her SPF 15 moisturizer, she began to dust the powdery white coral sand off her hands and gather up her book, her tote bag, her empty coffee cup and her beach towel.

"You're not leaving?" protested the redhead beside her. "I wanted you to meet Joey and Pete and the mob—they're super great, but Pete's date couldn't come at the last minute, so he came stag. Pete's twenty-four and a half. He drives an Alpha Romeo and owns this great condo in Aspen."

The young woman had started talking when she'd first plopped down in the next lounge and hadn't paused for breath. Daisy gathered that one of the studs cavorting on the beach was hers, and she'd been assigned the task of scouting out any unattached and presentable females at the resort. When a few distracted "um-hmms" hadn't turned her off, Daisy had considered slipping into her other personality. She'd worked long and hard to perfect the cool aloof facade that invariably worked like a charm, shedding over-friendly approaches like a duck sheds water.

Somehow she didn't think it would work with this bubbly young thing. "Sorry—I've already made plans to borrow a bicycle and go exploring the ruins." She would have invented a case of Montezuma's revenge to keep from spending the day romping around with a group of overanimated Ken and Barbie dolls.

"Oh. You've got a guy, then."

"No."

The glowy-faced redhead stared at her. "You mean you're going *alone?*"

Daisy shrugged. "I much prefer alone."

"Chic! Oh, wow!"

Daisy hadn't been trying for the Garbo effect, honestly. It was just that this friendly little puppy refused to take no for an answer. Having to fend off the waiters and the hotel's enthusiastic recreational directors was bad enough without the guests starting in on her.

Five minutes after Daisy had climbed out of the taxi two days before, still in shock from traveling more than a hundred kilometers in less than an hour on a narrow potholed road through the jungle, one of the rec directors had taken on the task of trying to match her up with another single—some tall, sandy-haired character with stainless-steel eyes and a face like a beardless young Abe Lincoln.

She had politely declined and had managed to dodge the resident matchmakers ever since. Now, gathering her belongings, she was more concerned with the best way to lever herself up out of the molded plastic chaise that had buried itself in the sand.

"Be sure you're back in time for the mixer in the Big Palapa tonight," the nubile Aphrodite in the thong bikini reminded her. "We could meet you there. They've got live music tonight."

"Sorry," said Daisy as she tested the strength of her legs against the weight of her body and the awkward angle to be negotiated. "I've made plans to watch the fungus grow on the grout in the bathroom."

"Huh?"

Daisy relented. It wasn't in her to deliberately hurt a child, even a voluptuous little airhead like this one, who could pop up and down out of these fiendish devices with no effort at all.

That didn't mean she was going to let herself be drawn into their games. She was no good at games. Never had been. "Thanks—I'll make a note of it." Settling her hat on her head, she shoved her oversize sunglasses back up her short nose, buttoned the black-and-white medallion-print overshirt Cora Joan had given her for the occasion and contemplated the next hurdle. There was simply no graceful way to get out of one of these things unless you were a teenager or an acrobat. Especially with her young friend watching her like a blue-eyed hawk.

"Wow, that's a great pair of earrings you're wearing! Did ya get 'em around here?"

"Hmm? No, in the States," Daisy murmured, wondering if she could tip the thing and roll over onto all fours.

"Oh, look, there's Pete now—isn't he great-looking? If it weren't for Joey, I'd go for him myself."

Daisy looked. The bronzed god in the French bathing trunks looked nearly young enough to be her son. Dammit, she didn't need this. It was depressing enough not to be able to get out of this confounded torture device!

"So have him washed and brought to my tent," she muttered as she lunged to her feet, wavered a moment, and then lurched forward half a dozen steps until she'd regained her balance.

The first thing she was going to do when she got home was make an appointment with her chiropractor. The second thing was murder her friend for booking her into a place like this. Club Caribe Azul. A tropical resort, Cora had said. Nothing to do but eat and sleep and check out the local craftsmen.

Ha! Club Coochie-Coo was more like it. The Garden of Eden with a recreational director. There weren't any local craftsmen. There weren't any local anythings! The hotel was plopped down in the middle of nowhere, with salt water on one side and swampy jungle on the other, and there wasn't even a blasted telephone closer than a hundred miles—or kilometers—whatever!

Granted, the scenery wasn't bad—in fact, it was lovely. And the weather was guaranteed in writing to be perfect. But the place was swarming with couples. It was a regular Noah's ark! And there was that incessant taped music that came over the loudspeaker. She was a captive audience of one in a world of twos, and she wasn't at all sure she was going to be able to stick it out the full two weeks.

Following the convoluted system of breezeways that led to her room, Daisy had to admit that the place wasn't all bad. The food was pretty good. Great, actually. If she were Robinson Crusoe and Friday never came, she would probably even enjoy it.

With the tennis courts on one side of the narrow walk and a thick bank of oleander on the other, she

nearly collided with a couple who were either new-
lyweds or Siamese twins. Ducking her head, she murmured an apology, but she might as well not have
bothered. For all those two cared, they were alone on
the planet.

God, was I ever that bad? I couldn't have been!

If Daisy had a besetting sin—and she had several,
she was the first to admit—it was her deep-seated
compulsion for privacy. Cora Joan Smith, the business partner who had practically bludgeoned her into
taking a vacation and booked her into this place, had
claimed that the polished facade she put on with her
makeup each morning was a cover-up for the real Daisy
Valentine, and that people who were afraid to allow
their real selves to show through eventually cracked.

Cora claimed that underneath all that hard-boiled
glitter, the real Daisy Valentine was shy, sensitive and
insecure.

Balderdash. Daisy had passed off that remark as she
did all others that came too close to the mark, with a
flippant comeback. "Rea-lly?" she'd drawled. "Sorry
to disillusion you, love, but what you see is that you
get. Like an onion. No matter how many layers you
peel away, you're not going to find shy and sensitive—
all you'll find is more onion."

Which was true, she told herself. She was what she
was—no more, no less. A thirty-eight-year-old divorcée, co-owner of a small reasonably successful hand-
made-jewelry   boutique—workaholic,   live-aloner,
adequate cook and fair amateur painter. If she hadn't
taken a vacation in more years than she could remember, it was only because she'd had neither the time nor
the money. Building a new life on the ruins of an old

one took more than guts—it took time, energy and a good line of credit. And if she happened to have taken on a rather hard polish in the process, all the better. Onions might get peeled, but diamonds seldom got scratched.

"Real whiz with metaphors, aren't you?" she muttered as she fit her key into the lock of 122D.

"¿Excúseme, señora?" said the boy in the white uniform, who was just leaving the room next door with his cleaning cart.

"Nothing—that is, *nada,*" Daisy said quickly. The boy smiled the smile of a Reubens cherub and went about his business, and Daisy locked herself inside, kicked off her sandals, dropped her sandy tote bag on the table, and sighed.

And then frowned. What had she said to him? She was pretty sure *nada* was the word she'd sought, but in this neck of the woods, language books weren't much use. Her Spanish was strictly high-school variety, and that was so long ago it was probably obsolete. Half the staff spoke some obscure Mayan dialect, and even those who claimed to speak Spanish didn't sound at all like anything she'd read in her little pocket-size Berlitz "new and revised" bilingual dictionary.

It was a challenge, she'd told herself that first day when she'd had to try to convince a non-English-speaking waiter that no, she wasn't waiting for anyone, and yes, she did want a table for one, and no, the gentleman behind the newspaper who was also obviously alone at the next table was not hers, thanks all the same.

On the other hand, Daisy Valentine had not come to Club Coochie-Coo to be challenged. She had come to relax. And she was damned well *going* to relax, if it killed her!

The only bicycle left was a boy's model, painted in the hotel's rather unfortunate colors, which were burnt orange and strawberry-ice-cream pink. And it was obviously built for someone whose legs ended at the knee. Daisy's went all the way up—to her armpits, according to her ex-husband, who was five foot six and had quickly come to resent Daisy's five ten.

The unpaved path immediately behind the hotel that led off through the jungle was obviously not meant for tourists' eyes. The first thing she saw was a dump. Idly swatting mosquitoes, she pushed aside two cracked plastic chaise lounges and uncovered a . . . totem pole? At least the beginnings of one.

It looked like mahogany. It also looked much larger than she'd first thought. What a great display piece, if she could only get it back to the shop. How much could it weigh? A hundred pounds? A thousand?

"I doubt if it'll fit in your luggage," came a dry masculine comment from behind her.

She spun around, nearly tripping over her bicycle in the process. It was the newspaper recluse. The one with the crooked nose, the stubborn jaw, the prominent cheekbones and the stainless-steel eyes. Add to that, she thought now, the mouth of a sensual cynic.

A sensual cynic? Daisy, you've had too many mango daiquiries! Hastily she tried for her usual cover, but this time she wasn't entirely successful. "I wasn't thinking that," she snapped.

"What were you thinking? About getting it through customs?"

"Would it be a problem? If I was, that is. Not that I was."

"See the carving?" Someone had obviously made an aborted attempt to carve a grotesque mask on the base, probably intending it as a mate for the five others that graced the front entrance of the hotel. "Can you prove it's not a valuable archeological artifact?" he asked, as a sudden gust of warm wind whipped his khakis and white shirt distractingly against his body.

Thank goodness for sunglasses, because Daisy couldn't help but stare. The man was built like a...like a man *should* be built. "Can customs prove it is?"

"They don't have to. When in doubt, it's easier to say no."

She shrugged. No one in his right mind would have tried to lug home half a ton of dead wood for a souvenir, anyway. It was only a thought. With a glance at the sky, which was rapidly clouding over, she resettled her Panama hat and prepared to ride off.

"It's going to rain," said Steel Eyes.

"It usually does . . . eventually."

"You don't mind getting wet?"

She gave him a practiced look that had left more than one man wondering if he had spinach between his front teeth. Then, with only the slightest wobble, she wheeled off down the narrow jungle path, ignoring the mosquito that was prepared to drill into her jugular. Ignoring the way her knees bumped against the handlebars.

And ignoring the feeling that she'd just met a man who didn't give a hoot in hades whether or not she owned her own house, her own business, and had just turned down an introduction to a nubile Arnold

Schwarzenegger who drove an Alpha Romeo and had a face like Rob Lowe.

"So who needs a middle-aged Scrooge who hides behind newspapers, anyway?" Daisy muttered as she tried to pretend she didn't look perfectly ridiculous on a bicycle that was much too small for her, racing furiously off down a bumpy road to nowhere.

Four hours later, Gardiner was on his way to the TV room. The single set in the entire complex happened to be located in the only place on the premises where a man could get a cup of coffee day or night. Good coffee. Damned fine coffee, in fact. For all its faults, there were several things the place had going for it, not the least of which was its proximity to two fine ruins he had yet to visit.

On his way back to his room with his brimming cup, he veered by the open-air lobby with the idea of signing up for tomorrow's trip to Cobá. He had meant to go by earlier, but had fallen asleep in his room and just awakened.

The rec director's office was closed, as it had been the other times he'd tried. There had to be a schedule around this place—hotels didn't run themselves haphazardly—but so far, he hadn't managed to figure it out. The activities list was posted in the lobby, but signing up was a problem. Where? When?

There was no one at all in the lobby, not even the desk clerk. He could hear sounds of laughter coming from the big thatched roof pavilion near the pool. Obviously the guests were enjoying another one of those games designed to mix, mingle and embarrass all concerned to the maximum allowed by law.

Feeling old and out of sorts, he scanned the hand-written schedule that listed weekly activities, from jungle walks to bike tours to folk dances to something they called a newlywed game. He had just turned to go when he heard someone slogging up the three stone steps behind him.

He turned and spoke before thinking. "What the devil happened to you?"

She was soaked to the skin—a skin that showed clearly through her pale yellow shirt and even through the band of lacy bra underneath. That ridiculous lop-sided Panama hat had lost its shape and now drooped unevenly, exposing a dark fringe of hair and a pair of large dark eyes that could have easily ignited a fire if she hadn't been so wet. And so tired. And so cold.

"Want some coffee?" It was purely an impulse. Gardiner wasn't given to impulses. "Wait here—no, you'll freeze. Tell me your room number and I'll bring it to you."

There was no such thing as room service. Free bar service, and free food when the dining room happened to be open, but no room service. Even paradise had its shortcomings.

Gardiner saw her eyes go longingly toward his cup of now lukewarm coffee. "No thanks," she said. "I know where to get it."

He shrugged. It had been an impulse, that was all. All he was offering was a cup of coffee. "Sure—no problem. Uh, the room's full of sports fans watching a game—you might want to throw on another shirt before you go in there."

She stared at him, and then she looked down the long, modestly curved length of her own body. Gar-

diner would have been less than human if he hadn't
enjoyed her shocked reaction when she discovered that
not only was she wet—she was clingingly, revealingly
wet.

"Oh, Lordy—122D," she mumbled, and he had to
ask her to repeat it.

"It's 122D! Past the tennis courts, facing the jungle, not the beach. Uh, two sugars and two creamers,
please—if you don't mind?"

He paused long enough to watch her hurry away, her
elegant legs spattered with mud and leaves, her thin
back ramrod stiff. It occurred to him that if she could
have stopped shivering long enough to put on a layer
of makeup, she'd probably have enjoyed sauntering
into a room full of men in her see-through shirt.

Georgia would have made the most of it—that was
just the sort of thing she'd done time after time. And
time after time, he'd fallen for it.

There were two jugs of coffee. He picked up the
fullest one and filled two tall cups, then grabbed a
handful of additives and stuffed them into his pocket.
It wasn't hard to calculate the location of 122D. His
own room was 223D. Given the layout, which was
simple enough, it had to be one flight down and one
door along from his. He'd probably have passed her
going and coming except for the fact that he'd quickly
discovered a service corridor and used it to go and
come so as to avoid the other guests.

She cracked the door open at his knock and reached
out a hand.

"Thank you very much."

"Don't mention it. Did you want anything to eat?
The dining room's still open."

"I'm not hungry. Thanks."

Her teeth were chattering. Beach hotels on the Caribbean weren't exactly geared for cold weather. There were wooden louvres to close over the windows, but no glass. No heat, no blankets, either.

"Look, why not come out and get a bowl of hot soup. It's not bad tonight." He could probably talk the management into letting him bring her supper to her room, but a man had to draw the line somewhere. The woman was nothing to him. If she had no better sense than to go haring off on a bike in the middle of a monsoon, that was no skin off his—

"Thank you, I think I will."

"What?"

"I'll have the coffee first, though. Thank you very much for bringing it. It was . . . thoughtful of you."

The door closed softly in his face before Gardiner could utter a protest—not that he knew what he was protesting. He'd done his good deed for the day. Now he could either relax with his book or take a walk on the beach, or join the revelry under the Big Palapa.

He shuddered at the thought. And reading was out. Some idiot with a tape deck and a cheap sound system insisted on broadcasting the kind of noise that passed for music among the hearing impaired and the criminally tone deaf.

Still, it was too early to turn in, even if he could have tuned out the noise. He'd already eaten—out of boredom rather than hunger.

But he hadn't had dessert. Besides that, he had a sweater. A wool pullover. And he'd bet his bottom dollar that Legs hadn't brought one along, else she would have been wearing it when she'd opened her door.

Taking the stairs two at a time, Gardiner whistled cheerfully, telling himself that he'd grab a bite of whatever sweet looked best on the nightly buffet, hand over the sweater and leave. He might stroll down the beach, after all—there was a moon tonight. In a week and a half, he'd be back in Raleigh, wading through slush to get to his classes, fighting off a head cold more than likely, and threatening his eight-year-old pickup with a crowbar when it refused to start.

By the time Daisy's teeth had stopped chattering, she realized she was famished. The food was one of the best things about the place—the food and that incredible turquoise water. And the soft white sand that stayed cool no matter how brightly the sun shone. And the birds—Lord yes, the birds! Tomorrow she was going to see if the rec director had a bird book. Before the rain had started coming down in buckets, she'd seen blue-and-green ones, black-and-yellow ones, and some beauties with salmon-pink breasts and dark backs that were so tame they'd perched on a power line right over her head for the longest time.

Hanging her wet jeans over the shower rod, and her shirt and bra over a chair back, she changed quickly into a pair of thick white socks, white duck pants, and her black-and-white medallion-print shirt over a T-shirt. Layering was the best she could do—the travel agent had assured her it would be deliciously warm and sunny her whole stay, and she'd been gullible enough to believe her.

He was standing outside the dining room when she spotted him. Damn! She'd understood him to say he had already eaten tonight. By the time she reached the door, skirting past the noisy group around the pool and the even noiser one under the Big Palapa, he was nowhere in sight.

"Thmoking or no-thmoking, theñorita?" asked the four-and-a-half-foot-tall maître d'.

"No-thmo—that is non-smoking," she murmured.

"Same for me," said Steel Eyes, who'd been studying the bill of fare when she'd come in.

"Ahhh," said the Mayan matchmaker, beaming. "¿Dos, no? Tonight we serve..." and then he rattled off something in an incomprehensible blend of Spanish and Mayan, and Daisy panicked.

"Soup! I only want soup—please?"

"Sopa de mariscos, sopa de..."

"Just say si," Gardiner instructed her quietly, and took her arm to follow the waiter who had appeared beside them.

"You speak Spanish?" she asked after he'd seated her at a table for four beside the window.

"Enough to get by. Hold on—I'll get you some soup and bread, and maybe some salad, okay?"

The dining room was nearly deserted. She should have insisted on her own table, but at the moment, she lacked the strength to protest.

Daisy watched the tall lean man as he crossed the room. It occurred to her that he looked out of place among the sunburned vacationers she'd seen so far. He wasn't tanned. He wasn't wearing colorful resort wear. He made no effort to blend in.

It also occurred to her that the other men looked weaker, less significant, by comparison. She was still mulling over that rather surprising notion when he brought her a bowl of steaming seafood chowder and several chunks of the wonderful bread that accompanied all the meals.

Before she could thank him, he was gone again, to return a few moments later with another plate filled with four different kinds of dessert.

Hastily swallowing a mouthful of delectable soup, she said, "Oh, but I don't eat desserts—thank you, though."

He looked at her blankly for an instant, and then said, "These are mine."

To cover her embarrassment, Daisy glanced around for the waiter who hovered just out of reach. "Could I please have some butter?"

The boy smiled at her.

"Butter?" she repeated, a little louder. When he made no move, she held up a piece of dry bread.

He continued to beam at her, and she swore mildly under her breath. She was digging in her purse for her bilingual dictionary when the man across from her said quietly, *"Mantequilla, por favor."*

"¡Ah, si!"

The Mayan cherub moved fast enough when *he* spoke, she thought rancorously. Of course, speaking the language helped. Reluctantly she thanked him again. It was getting to be a habit—one she didn't care for. It wasn't her nature to be dependent—not any longer.

"No problem. Most of them speak more English than they let on. I think it's a game kids like to play with grownups the world over."

"You're probably right. I'm embarrassed that I've forgotten what little I learned in school."

"Most people do that, too, unless there's a reason to remember. The odd fact or two sticks—irrelevant ones, usually."

He smiled, and Daisy revised her opinion of his looks. The man would never be considered handsome in the traditional sense, but there was definitely something about him that warranted a second look. And a third.

Not until he had excused himself and risen to go did it occur to her that she didn't even know his name. Nor he hers.

Two

———

It continued to rain in paradise. And rain, and rain, and rain. Not even the persistent sound system could compete with the steady drone of rain on tile roofs, on coral-embedded patios and hard-packed limestone ground.

The cleaning staff of teenage Mexican boys gave up their stiffly starched whites to run around barefoot in plastic garbage-bag ponchos, but their shy greetings were no less cheerful. As she dashed back and forth to the dining room for meals, Daisy enjoyed practicing her inadequate Spanish on them.

"Buen's dias, s'ñorita."

"Buenos dias, señor—uh, *muchacho*—uh . . ." No, not boy. That sounded too patronizing.

"Buen's tardes, s'ñorita."

"Buenas tardes, amigo." Oh, God, that was too forward. The child wasn't a friend—she didn't even know his name.

"Buen's noches, s'ñorita."

"Buenas noches," she chimed back with a big smile.

And got one in return.

Gardiner observed all this. He enjoyed watching the rain on the jungle and on the water. If that occasionally included watching his long-stemmed neighbor practice charming the native populace, where was the harm? He was immune. Besides, he wouldn't get anywhere with a woman like her, even if he weren't.

Daisy read until the wee hours three nights in a row, and barely made breakfast as a result. Ignoring the grumblings and complaints about the weather she heard all around her, she had actually begun to enjoy herself. The college crew had moved on, and another bus load of tourists had come in from the airport at Cancun. There was a new barrage of comments on the cloudy skies.

"I thought this was supposed to be the dry season."

"My travel agent told me it *never* rains here in January. Hell, I left five feet of snow on the ground back in Detroit—and for *this?*"

The Big Palapa leaked a little. The individual palapas on the beach leaked a lot. The thatched roof of the bar leaked, too, but not enough to discourage the clientele. Gardiner was there, nursing his second Mexican beer of the day, when he saw her go by, headed for the beach. It was blowing a warm misty rain, and she was covered from midthigh up with garbage bags, one belted around her waist, a smaller one anchored with her indomitable Panama hat, but he'd have known those legs anywhere.

One thing he had discovered over the past few days of woman-watching was that his immunity wasn't quite as secure as he'd thought. The first day during a break in the showers he had watched with a prick of resentment as she picked her way over the rough coral on *his* private beach. The resentment was followed by a mild rush of satisfaction that someone else preferred it to the hotel's manicured grounds.

The second day he'd watched her sitting out on her miniscule patio, knees drawn up under her chin as she painted her toenails pale pink—and he'd gotten a rather uncomfortable reaction.

The third day he'd watched her eat grilled chicken drumsticks with her fingers, and he'd gotten so turned on he hadn't been able to leave his table for a full five minutes after she'd gone.

Now the crowd at the bar was beginning to get rowdy as the rain continued to fall. Gardiner nursed his beer, reminded of too many student gatherings on too many campuses. He'd always been too broke to hang out, but he had usually found a job there in his undergraduate years.

Downing the last of his drink, he turned to leave. He'd gotten into his mystery novel the night before— this would be a great afternoon to finish it.

Only somehow he found himself on the beach instead of back in his room. Ignoring the rain-muted beauty all around him, he began to walk. To the north lay the rougher stretch. He'd already explored it pretty thoroughly. Besides, it was empty.

Without conscious decision, he headed south.

There were one or two small condos along the palm-strewn sandy beach, huddled against the hotel property as if for protection against the encroaching jungle. Then there was nothing. Banana trees, swamps, several varieties of palm he had never seen before, and a few he had. The beach sand was washed away here and there, revealing the limestone bedrock. Bleached coral boulders lay toppled about and forgotten by past storms.

Litter was everywhere, some natural, some man-made. It was strange, wild and beautiful, and Gardiner told himself it was just the way he liked his beaches—deserted. But when he saw her, he knew himself for a liar.

Actually, he wasn't even certain it was she at first—it could easily have been a bag of garbage someone had tossed out that had washed up on the shore. She was sitting hunched over on a ruined palm frond with one leg curled under her and the opposite foot drawn up into her lap.

"Need any help?" He hadn't realized she hadn't heard him approach until she jumped and swore. On all that plastic, rain—even a light rain—must be noisy as the devil, he thought. "Sorry—I didn't mean to startle you."

Daisy yelped when her wet foot slipped out of her grasp. "Oh blast, I nearly had it!" Her mood disintegrated further when she peered up from under her drooping hat brim and saw who her intruder was. The last thing she needed was a pushy jerk with a superior attitude.

"Picked up a spur?"

At least the jerk kept his distance. Wearing a gray nylon windbreaker, plain black boxers and a pair of ancient gray deck shoes, he looked totally out of place against the colorful Caribbean setting. No sense of fashion whatsoever.

Oh? And which one of you is dressed in garbage bags? Daisy asked herself. Scowling, she continued to poke at the sole of her foot. "It's nothing—probably just a stone bruise."

"I could take a look for you."

"No thanks."

"Might save trouble down the line. Lord knows where the nearest medical help is."

"It's nothing—really." She glanced up, still scowling, and found herself staring at his mouth, waiting for it to move. Quickly she looked back down at her foot. So the man had interesting bone structure—so what?

"Were you looking for the shipwreck?"

Her gaze flew back up to his interesting bone structure. "There was a shipwreck? When?"

His lips twitched, and once more she found herself watching them. "Well, not recently. Supposed to be an old one along here somewhere."

"Probably more tourist hype. Like the weather."

Gardiner hunkered down beside her. He was beginning to enjoy himself for reasons he didn't care to examine too closely. Not that he wasn't wary—he'd never been comfortable with women. As for playing the kind of games they seemed to expect from men, he wouldn't know how to make the first move even if he wanted to.

All the same, here he was. And there she was. "This one's real," he said. "There was a book out ten or fifteen years back—before Quintana Roo was made a

state, when all this stretch along here was still a terri-
tory. The author claimed to have explored the area
pretty thoroughly. Said he heard tales about an old
shipwreck and followed them up, and sure enough,
there she was. According to the maps in the book, she
should be right around here somewhere.''

"If some author published a map to a shipwreck in
a book fifteen years ago, then I seriously doubt that
there's anything left of it by now. *If* it ever existed.''

Even in black plastic she looked good, he mused.
Soaking wet, with a limp straw hat pulled down over
her eyes and goose bumps on every exposed inch of
flesh, she looked entirely too good for comfort. *His*
comfort, that was. From the cut of her jaw, she was
definitely no pushover. On the other hand, there was
more than a hint of vulnerability about those soft naked lips of hers. Even in the rain, he'd have expected
full war paint from most women. Georgia wouldn't
have been caught dead without the stuff.

She was older than he'd first thought. There was a
tiny fan of creases at the outer edges of her chestnut-
brown eyes—another fine line across her forehead.
Nice. It made her more approachable. And if he wasn't
mistaken, there was a definite glint of silver in the inky
fringe that straggled out from under her hat.

Against his will, Gardiner found himself being
drawn, being touched—being attracted. "You're p-p-
probably a model," he stuttered, addressing his knee-
cap.

"Is that a question?" It wasn't the first time Daisy
had been asked if she were a model. An accident of
birth had given her cheekbones, small breasts and long
legs. Unfortunately, she hadn't realized they could be

assets until a few years ago. Nothing like the fury of a woman dumped to bring out that certain sparkle. A few make-over sessions, a bold new hairstyle, a brand-new wardrobe, and she'd been ready to leave her footprints on the backside of any man who dared to even speak to her. "No, I'm not—but thanks."

He shrugged and looked out across the water. Daisy was tempted to ask what he did for a living.

No, she wasn't. She wasn't interested in anything about the man.

Abruptly, she got to her feet, winced as she put her full weight on her right one, and leaned over to scoop up the bag of small treasures she'd found. Nice bits of bleached coral mostly, with a few hard brown things she suspected were seeds of some sort. Her mind had immediately pictured them entwined with sterling wires—or possibly a combination of metals.

Daisy didn't actually make the jewelry she sold in the shop, but after four years of scouting craft shows for interesting and attractive wares, she tended to see most things in terms of jewelry designs and displays. The junk she'd collected would make an interesting display.

She headed back to the hotel, sticking to the softer portions of the beach. The walking was easier. Even so, she knew she was limping, and it didn't help her disposition to know that *he* was right behind her. She felt self-conscious, and she hated the feeling. Sore feet didn't exactly go with the image she had spent four years carefully perfecting.

He was right behind her when she stepped up onto the paved walkway, his deck shoes gritting against the coral-embedded concrete. The rain had ceased, making her feel slightly foolish in her plastic shroud, but she tilted her head at an arrogant angle and strode off toward her section just as if every step weren't driving that wicked little spur deeper into the ball of her right foot.

Halfway along the tennis courts, he caught up with her. "Do you have an antiseptic?"

"No. Yes. Probably." Her medical supplies consisted of a couple of different brands of antacid and her brand-new reading glasses in case she started getting headaches.

"You can probably find something at the hotel store."

Practically at her door, she gave in to the pain and began to hobble. But then she turned to stare at him. "Hotel store. You mean *this hotel?*"

"Sure. It's tucked away in a sort of cul-de-sac behind a bunch of spare patio furniture near the main office. I'm not sure of the hours, but if you're lucky, you can find them open at least once or twice a day."

"And you think they might have something?"

"Hard to tell. It's small, and they carry a pretty weird selection of stock. Shall I stop by and see for you?"

No way, Sir Galahad. "No thanks—I'll check it out on my way to dinner. If I happen to need anything, that is."

"Sure. Better get it in shape, though—weather's going to come around tomorrow. You might want to take the bus tour to Cobá."

They had reached her door by then, and Daisy leaned against it, staring at the water that swirled up to within an inch of the outside corridor. The grounds, walled in against the jungle, were completely awash. She might have been alarmed, but no one else seemed to take it as anything out of the ordinary. As it was, she was merely fascinated. A platter-sized hibiscus blossom floated past, its deep rose petals undulating on the water as it eddied toward the corner.

"Cobá... That's one of the ruins, isn't it?"

"Mmm-hmm."

She stared after the floating blossom, carefully not looking at his rugged face or the length of tanned body exposed behind the half-open zipper of his billowing windbreaker. He was hairy, but not overly so. Muscular, but again, not overly so. Not like those young jocks who spent half their time lying on the beach and the other half flexing their muscles. "It's worth seeing," she murmured, and then, stricken with embarrassment, blurted, "The ruin, I mean! Is it worth seeing?"

"I dunno—I haven't seen it yet."

The flower disappeared around the corner and Daisy made up her mind on the spot. Tomorrow, if the roads weren't under water, she would see about getting herself to Tulum. Once she was sure he'd done Cobá, she might make the trip herself. No point in passing up any of the local attractions while she was here. On the other hand, she had no intention of barging into old Steel Eyes behind every pile of rocks.

The desk clerk arranged for her to take a taxi to the famous seaside Mayan ruin about half an hour's drive farther south. That way, she could stay as long as she liked without having to worry about keeping up with her group.

It irritated her that Steel Eyes had been right about the weather, but with the rain clouds gone and the standing water rapidly draining away, the pink-and-orange resort was once again glistening with Technicolor brilliance.

Daisy slathered on a heavy-duty moisturizing sunscreen and tugged her hat down over her head before gathering up a tote filled with watercolors, bottled drinking water—which she intended to use partly for painting—and some cookies and cheese. The little store had been open, and it had indeed carried an antiseptic for her foot.

She couldn't locate her Berlitz, but praying that her driver would have more English than she had Spanish, she tucked her currency conversion card into her bag and hurried along to the taxi area out in front.

It was a glittering, palm-rustling, bird-singing morning! In a fit of goodwill as she sped along the narrow highway, Daisy spared a hope that Steel Eyes was enjoying his bus trip to Cobá as much as she was enjoying her rackety taxi run to Tulum.

Once they pulled into the bustling little square outside the ruined city, she began making arrangements for the return trip.

"Can you come back for me at four this afternoon?" she asked.

"Afternoon," the driver repeated dutifully.

"You do understand English, don't you?"

"English." He nodded and smiled.

"Um—I need to get back to the hotel from Tulum?"

"*Si*, Tulum." He nodded and smiled some more.

This conversation didn't seem to be going anywhere in particular. She would have to trust to luck that he

understood more than he appeared to. The desk clerk
had told her the drivers all charged a flat rate for the
trip, and she took out her card and began figuring the
tip. Translating dollars into pesos was hard enough.
Translating percentages was out of the question.

The sun blistered down from a cloudless sky. She was
beginning to perspire. The driver stood patiently smiling, while several of his cohorts called out laughing remarks. In Spanish.

Hands trembling, Daisy counted out the amount
quoted by the clerk and rashly added half as much
more. Then she pointed at her wristwatch. "Four," she
repeated. "You understand four?"

"*Sí,* four."

A parrot could do as well, she thought hopelessly.
"You—" she jabbed a finger at his chest, and then at
her own "—me. Four. Right here." She pointed to the
ground and then said brightly, "Okay?"

"Hokay."

"Oh, God," she muttered, wondering if the man had
the least notion of anything she'd said. Shouldering her
bag, she took a moment to get her bearings, pur-
chased a ticket and climbed the stairs that led through
the wall into the archeological zone.

"He'll be back on time, you know," said a familiar
voice, and she nearly dropped her tote.

"You were listening!" she accused.

He shrugged.

"You didn't go to Cobá." That, too, was an accu-
sation.

"Neither did you."

"I thought I'd—that is . . ."

"Yeah, me too." His smile brought about a re-markable change as lean cheeks creased, slightly crooked white teeth gleamed, and a pair of steady stainless-steel eyes suddenly took on the warmth of old pewter.

"You going to follow one of the groups and listen to the spiel?" he asked.

"No, I'd rather see it by myself." She shifted her weight and edged under the slight shade of the only tree around. It was a sapling. The circle of shade was three feet in diameter. Her companion stood bareheaded in the blinding noonday sun.

"Me too. You like clockwise or counterclockwise?"

It took her a moment to answer, and when she said clockwise, he grinned and nodded.

Gardiner had seen the waggling movement of her forefinger as she mentally followed the hands of a clock. "Counter for me. See you back at the hotel, then," and he sauntered off, ignoring a discourse on the theories of the descending gods as he skirted a group of tourists clustered around their guide and fol-lowed a footpath to the right.

He had figured that if he suggested she go to Cobá, she would go to Tulum instead, leaving him free to go to Cobá with no distractions. He'd been right—she'd chosen Tulum. At the last minute, so had he. And Gardiner was *not* an impulsive man.

Daisy, telling herself she'd better make use of the shade for a few more minutes before she ventured out under the tropical sun, watched him stride away. He looked right at home in this setting, she thought, irri-tated again for no real reason. In his worn khaki pants and equally worn chambray shirt, he could easily have been an explorer. Or an adventurer. Or a soldier of fortune. He was probably an aluminum-siding salesman.

Wrenching her mind away from the sight of his lean masculine form, she focused her attention on the panorama before her. To think that some thousand-odd years ago, men had built a magnificent city here in what must surely be the most beautiful location anywhere in the world, and then disappeared without a trace.

A trace... A trace of gray. His hair was lighter than she'd thought at first—brown, with a glint of gold where the sun hit it. Actually there was more than a trace of gray. It was an elusive blend of silver, gold and bronze.

Reining her unruly thoughts back into line, Daisy reminded herself that there were still Mayans here on the peninsula, speaking the same dialect, planting the same crops and living in the same sort of thatched-roof houses their ancestors had built. Which meant that they'd hardly disappeared without a trace. Her driver could have been a Mayan for all she knew, a direct descendant of the very men and women who had built this fantastic walled city.

Her eyes took on a slightly unfocused look as she wondered what *his* name was, and who *he* was the direct descendant of. And what he was doing alone at a place like Club Coochie-Coo.

Oh, why the dickens was she wasting her valuable time? She should be painting, or soaking up culture— or at least showing some appreciation for an ancient city that was still breathtakingly lovely, for all it lay in ruins.

Twenty minutes later, after peering into an assortment of dark holes and climbing several sets of incredibly narrow stairs, Daisy found herself a flat shaded
rock in an archway in the surrounding outer wall and
got out her paints. Thirty minutes later, she was hum-
ming off-key and sloshing puddles of cerulean into a
wash of pale viridian in an attempt to duplicate the
delicate colors of the tropical sky.

Gardiner watched from his vantage place off to one
side. Hatless, he was probably being incinerated by the
sun, but with the breeze off the water, it wasn't too
painful. Yet.

Dammit, she was fascinating. One minute she came
off tough as old boots, the next she looked as vulnerable was somebody's kid sister. Whatever she was, she
was trouble. Women who looked like this one did—
who had the panache to come alone to a place like this,
to dress in a garbage bag with hubcap-sized earrings
and a hat that was so shabby only a woman who was
totally self-possessed would be caught dead in it—that
kind of woman was definitely off-limits to a middle-
aged math teacher whose hobbies were even duller than
his profession.

All the same, she was interesting to watch. She sat
flat on her butt, feet spread apart, paper laid out between her legs. With a thrust of an elbow and a sweep
of a long graceful hand, she moved in quick little flur-
ries and then grew still. Now and then she leaned back
and tilted her head at an angle to study what she'd
done.

A painter. Gardiner knew enough about art to fill a
thimble. Almost. According to his old man, art was the
nudes on the calendars that used to decorate the walls

of the garage where he played checkers when his lungs had gotten too bad for him to work anymore.

But then, the old man had been wrong about a lot of things, including the odds on Gardiner's making it through school. He'd not only made it through, he'd gone back to teach. Of the five Gentry brothers, Gardiner was the only one who had done what he'd set out to do. Both he and Bill had fought in Vietnam. Bill had continued to fight the war for seventeen years after it ended. He'd finally bought it somewhere in a Central American jungle.

Jeff had been sentenced to twelve years in prison for manslaughter after a drunken brawl. He was out after three, trying to live with his conscience and patch up his marriage. Edgar had died in a cave-in seven years ago, and Jimmy, the baby, who'd been going to set Nashville on its ear, was driving an eighteen-wheeler and trying to support a seventeen-year-old wife and a three-year-old daughter.

The Gentries weren't good with women. There had been no chance to learn at home, and the few times any one of them had gotten involved, it had turned out badly.

Georgia had been smart to get out before she'd gotten in any deeper. Gardiner didn't go around bragging about his family, but then, he didn't try to hide them, either. He'd laid it out for her before he'd asked her to marry him. Actually he had never gotten around to asking her, which was how he'd ended up in Mexico on a honeymoon for one.

Still, he'd made a point of setting her straight when she had seemed to think he'd been born to tweed, elbow patches and faculty teas. The truth was, he'd been born to coal mines, corn liquor and disability payments. They only reason he'd made it out of there was because he was tougher than any of them had given him credit for being.

And he was a quick study. He only had to learn a lesson once.

A flock of chattering shutter-clicking tourists invaded his perch, and Gardiner levered himself up and made his way diagonally down the crumbling terraces to where the long-stemmed beauty was still hunched over her work. What the hell—he was on vacation. Nothing that happened on vacation was connected in any way to reality.

"Hello again. My name's Gardiner Gentry—would you care to have a d-d-drink with me?" Dammit, he wasn't nervous! She simply wasn't that important to him!

Daisy dropped her brush, hastily slid a sheet of paper over her painting and stared up at him with a pair of wary eyes. "I brought my own supply, but thanks, anyway."

One dark level brow lifted and settled back down. "No problem. I just wasn't sure if you had a spare bottle."

"I don't need a . . ."

She reached for the plastic bottle she'd been sipping on, painting with, wetting down paper with, and once even drenching her handkerchief to lay over the back of her neck. It held about half an inch of tepid tasteless water.

Reaching into his pack, Gardiner Gentry drew out a couple of sweaty cans of soda. Nothing in recent memory had looked quite so good to her.

"Actually, I am rather thirsty. Um, Daisy Valentine."

He did that thing with his eyebrow again, and Daisy stared, fascinated in spite of the discomfort that was just now making itself felt. Her legs were cramped, her bottom was paralyzed, and her back was slowly cracking in three separate places.

"I beg your pardon?" he said.

"You do?"

"The V-V-Valentine thing?"

"It's my name," she said through clenched teeth. "Daisy Valentine." If he made a single wisecrack, she was going to flatten him. If she hadn't been so hurt when Beau had divorced her, she'd have kept his name—Daisy Monclare never raised any eyebrows.

But she had been, and so she'd gone back to her maiden name. There was nothing actually wrong with it once all the adolescent jokes were out of everyone's system. As a businesswoman she'd learned that a memorable name could even be an asset.

"They've got a pretty decent selection over across the way, Ms. Valentine. Are you hungry?"

"I brought cheese and cookies with me." And now, of course she had to offer to share them.

She spread her small feast over the rock, after first clearing away her painting gear. Gardiner popped the tops of the cans, dug three small boxes of raisins from his pack and added them to the pile, and while he made himself comfortable on the sunny side of the rock, Daisy surreptitiously stretched first one leg and then the other, working out the morning's accumulation of kinks.

By the time they'd eaten everything in sight, she knew a little more about him. She knew, for instance, that he was neither a soldier of fortune nor an aluminum-siding salesman; he was a college professor. Which made her, with her high-school diploma, feel slightly inadequate—but then, that was her problem, not his. His subject was mathematics, which didn't help any, either, and he spoke at least one additional language. She vowed to locate her Berlitz that very night and read it through cover to cover before she went to sleep.

But he was nice. He had nice eyes. And she thought he was rather shy, although why any man with all he had going for him should be shy was beyond her. Ah, well, she'd be the last one to claim to understand the male animal and his ego.

"Did you go up into the *castillo?*" he asked after they'd eaten everything in sight, and she shook her head.

"Want to give it a try?" He carefully flattened the raisin boxes and shoved them back in his pack. She'd emptied two of them.

"Not particularly."

"The view's pretty spectacular."

"I can imagine. I climbed up on that thingamabob between the two big whatchamacallits."

Gardiner's eyes danced, but he didn't smile. "Then I guess you got pretty much the same impact. One whatchamacallit's pretty much like another one, huh?"

She didn't want to tell him her foot was throbbing and have him say I-told-you-so. "I really believe one can get a better perspective from a distance."

Actually, she was intrigued by the scent of his body, and embarrassed by the rather remarkable effect it was having on her libido. She was thirty-eight years old, for pity's sake. Her hormones had long since gotten tired of waiting around for something to happen. They'd given up on her.

"You familiar with the local reptile population?"

In the process of repacking her tote, Daisy shot him a narrowed glance. "You mean like snakes?"

"And lizards."

Uneasily, she twisted around to glance behind her. The jungle was at her back, with a narrow footpath leading away from the walled site. Snakes? "Are there any poisonous ones around here?"

"I'm not sure, but there's one that's sunning about three feet behind your, uh, back, and it's—"

Daisy didn't wait to hear the end of his statement. With all the grace of a panic-stricken giraffe, she launched herself out of the arch and onto a clear patch of grass.

"You scared him off," Gardiner said calmly. He hadn't moved an inch.

"Look, if this is your idea of a joke..."

"No joke. It was just a good sized iguana—nice coloring, too. I thought you might like a closer look, but if you aren't interested in the species..."

There was nothing in his demeanor to indicate that he was enjoying a joke at her expense. After several moments, Daisy smiled. And then she chuckled aloud. All right, so today was her day for acting the fool. It was hardly his fault that she had just discovered that under a tropical sun in the middle of January, she could be turned on by the simple scent of healthy male sweat and freshly laundered cottons. Nor was it his fault that, while she adored all things with feathers and tolerated most things with fur, she had never been able to abide anything with scales that crawled on its belly.

Gardiner stood up and reached out a hand to help her up. Unthinkingly, she took it.

The sun was instantly eclipsed. A city that had endured for a thousand years suddenly ceased to exist as startled brown eyes stared into startled gray ones.

Centuries spun past before it occurred to Daisy that he was still holding her hand. She tugged hers away and backed up one step, and then another one. "Yes—that is, thanks. My ride..."

Gardiner nodded. It was not quite three—her ride was scheduled for four. He didn't know why she was running away, but he was damned glad she was. Because if she hadn't, he'd have had to. And at the moment, he wasn't sure he had the coordination to put one foot in front of the other.

Three

Gardiner waited until she'd left in her own taxi before waving over another one. He could have saved himself a bushel of pesos by sharing, but he'd have walked back first.

All the way back to the hotel he lectured himself for following up one damned fool blunder with another. He was supposed to be a learned man—in one or two areas, at least. In the area of human relations, especially those of the female variety, he was a total nonstarter.

The near miss with Georgia he discounted. It had been a fluke. A friend on the faculty had once told him that he had a reputation among the female members of the staff for being a hard nut to crack. Embarrassed, he'd brushed it off and soon forgotten it.

That is, until Georgia Ann Riggs, third-year student at a nearby women's college and a frequent visitor on campus, had dropped her purse at his feet, and he'd been forced to crawl around on his hands and knees helping her gather up her belongings.

Not until much later had he learned that it had been no accident. She'd done it on a dare, and having succeeded that far, had decided to crack the hardest nut on campus.

He'd been a pushover. Sexually, they weren't even in the same league. Not that he'd realized it at the time, of course—hell, he was no virgin. But it had been Georgia who'd led the way. A bewitching aggressor, she had seduced and instructed with such subtle expertise that he'd honestly thought he was God's gift to womankind.

It couldn't have lasted much longer, although he hadn't seen it that way at the time. She'd insisted on accompanying him to a few faculty functions, and lying in bed later, she had teased away his misgivings over their relative roles as teacher and student.

She was good at teasing. He'd been so besotted by that time he'd have jumped through burning hoops for her. Damned near had!

He'd taken it for granted that they would be married. In the heat of a pretty torrid moment, she'd claimed to love everything about him, and he had been stammering so much, he couldn't get out a coherent word, much less a proposal.

But he'd thought marriage was a given. They'd been practically living together, after all. If she had suggested they run off and join a circus, he'd probably have gone right along with the idea at that point. He'd bought her a ring that had cost more than he could afford, and she'd slipped it onto her right hand and mentioned earrings.

As a wedding gift, he'd thought.

He had made arrangements for the trip to a Mexican resort, and she'd claimed to love the sound of it, as long as it was close to a lot of good shops. He'd been thinking more in terms of archeological sites, but the travel agent promised him his bride would adore nearby Cancun.

It was only when he'd driven her out to the country to look at an old farmhouse he had considered buying that she'd begun to back off.

Deep down he must have sensed all along that it wasn't going to work out. The sex was great, but there was the difference in their ages—she was barely twenty-two, he was forty-one. She was voluptuous, beautiful and wildly popular; he was staid, respected by his colleagues, but not even his own mother, if she'd lived, could have called him handsome. As for their backgrounds, their tastes, their values and just about everything else measurable, there was simply no meeting ground. The coed had cracked the tough nut—probably won a few bets along the way—and the professor had gotten himself an education.

Oh, he'd gone through all the usual stages when she'd laughed in his face and walked out. Disbelief, anger, hurt. And finally, relief. Like walking five miles in a pair of three-hundred-dollar shoes that were a size too small. And then taking them off.

Now he supposed if he felt anything at all, it was gratitude. She had taught him a lot. At least now he knew his limitations.

Back at the hotel, Gardiner paid off the cabdriver and loped up the three steps to the open lobby. He had time to finish his book, enjoy a swim and a shower, and maybe a walk on the beach before dinner. And this time he'd make damned sure he had the beach to himself before he set out.

Castle, temple, or coast-guard station? Daisy studied the three watercolors lined up against the wall and wished she had taken time to find out what each building was. That was her problem—one of her problems. She was always rushing into things without enough information. An impression gatherer rather than a fact gatherer, according to Cora Joan, who relied on Daisy to scout out craftsmen, to select stock, to arrange the displays and plan the advertising, but who wouldn't have let her touch the books with a ten-foot pole.

Okay, she'd compromise and call it the coast-guard station of the descending gods, to be on the safe side. It overlooked the sea, and it had a bas-relief of a pot-bellied creature in a starched loincloth standing on his head. Besides, it wasn't as if anyone would ever see it. She might use one or two sketches as backgrounds for a display, and then they would be thumbtacked to her kitchen wall along with her other sketches until they curled up and turned yellow.

Scribbling a few pertinent bits of data on the back of each sketch, she tossed them aside and began pawing through her remaining clean clothes for something to wear to dinner. Thank goodness for a wash-and-wear hairstyle! She'd gone from an overlong ponytail to a ragged urchin's cut four years ago only because Beau had always hated her in short hair. Since then it had occurred to her more than once that it was one of the few things she had to thank him for.

She selected white duck pants, an oversize white silk shirt, and her malachite jewelry—big blobs of oxidized silver worked around rough slabs of blue-green stone, with crude brass and sterling chains. The earrings alone weighed a ton, but she loved them.

Besides, they worked for her. Like the haircut and the attitude she'd cultivated. No longer was she ignored by shop clerks, bank tellers and the world in general. Daisy Monclare had been a doormat. Daisy Valentine and her attitude were a force to be reckoned with.

There had been a new mob just checking in when she'd come through the lobby. Attitude hadn't helped her there—she'd had to elbow and apologize her way through. The touching hadn't bothered her. That close-quarters kind seldom did. It was the other kind she couldn't abide—the kind where people opened you up and touched what was inside. That was the kind that could hurt. But that didn't happen anymore—not since she'd cultivated her attitude.

Gardiner Gentry had come too close today. They'd laughed together, and she'd noticed things about him—his hands, for instance. He had wide palms with long strong fingers. Capable sensitive hands, she'd thought, and then scoffed at herself for being an idiot.

All the same, it was too easy to imagine those hands touching her. When he'd helped her up, she had gone into shock for a moment. It had been the craziest feeling—like currents of electricity flowing back and forth, sealing them together. It had left her gasping for breath. For all she knew, she'd been standing there with her mouth gaping open.

Cora Joan kept telling her it was time to start dating again. Maybe she should, just to develop a little natural resistance so that she wouldn't be caught off guard again.

That is if she could find anyone who was interested in dating a thirty-eight-year-old retread. For six months after Beau had told her that he wanted a divorce—that he was ready to start a family now that his career was precisely where he wanted it, but that at her age, she wasn't a very good bet—Daisy had cried. For six solid months she had cried!

Granted, she was seven years older than Beau—the marriage had been another of her act-now-think-later decisions. But she certainly wasn't over the hill. Plenty of women in their late thirties had babies. And at that time, she'd been only in her middle thirties.

Of course, she hadn't known then about all his little 'side interests.' The day after their no-fault divorce was final, Beau had married one of those interests, and Daisy had blown her nose, mopped her eyes and started construction on the new improved, nonbreakable Daisy Valentine.

And no blasted gray-eyed, bony-faced, crooked-smiling schoolteacher was going to threaten her security! Hard-boiled worked. Hard-boiled put men off, and when they couldn't get close, they couldn't turn your life upside down. She might not have a college degree, but at least she'd learned that much.

Four hours later she strolled into the crowded dining room, looking as haughty as five-foot-ten with cheekbones and a French haircut could possibly look.

She imagined herself on a runway, gazing in deadly bored fashion above the heads of the crowd.

"Una mesa para uno, por favor," she drawled in her best Berlitz.

The little book was great for memorizing useful phrases, all right. It just wasn't much good when it came to translating responses given in a rapid-fire burst of Mayan-Spanish.

"Just say yes," came a familiar voice near her left ear.

"I *beg* your pardon." But she was already losing altitude. Impossible not to when he was standing so close, his eyes glinting warmly and a grin tugging at the corners of his stern mouth.

"The locusts have descended. I overheard one of the kitchen crew saying they're about to run out of the beef and the seviche, and there's still a mob outside waiting to get in."

From that point on, Gardiner and Daisy joined forces. At least for meals. Daisy told herself it was the only sensible thing to do in light of the fact that, with the hotel now filled to capacity, they both felt guilty claiming two entire tables when a single one would have sufficed.

The moon was just rising when they strolled outside, stuffed to the gills, that first night. A small band was playing out on the patio. "We c-c-could sit and watch for a while if you'd like to," Gardiner said, as if it didn't matter one way or another to him. "The band's not half b-bad."

Daisy shrugged. "Why not?" she asked carelessly. "It's a nice-enough evening." A nice-enough evening?

she thought, staring after him as he wove his way through the dancers. Palm trees silhouetted against an enormous tropical moon, the ocean lapping on soft white sands, a band playing fifties' oldies, and a handsome enigmatic man whose eyes seemed strangely luminous in the moonlight?

While she was still debating diving for the nearest cover, he headed for the bar. Within minutes, he was on his way back with a beer and a daiquiri. She didn't even care what kind it was.

She watched his approach. Did teaching math build shoulders like that? Did balancing equations give him that easy masculine grace?

In a sudden panic, she snatched the drink from his hand with a mumbled thanks and gulped half of it down, crushed ice and all, and then grabbed her forehead as pain slammed against her skull.

"Too cold, too fast?" he asked.

Stroking her temples, she nodded. "Whew! Ever since my first bite of ice cream—I must have been about two. You'd think I'd learn, wouldn't you?"

He only smiled and tapped his fingers on the table in time to the music.

She was afraid he would ask her to dance, but he didn't.

Perversely, she was disappointed.

After an hour had passed, she pretended a yawn and said, "It's getting late. You stay—they're just getting wound up good, from the looks of it." At least a dozen couples were dancing. There was one group playing bridge at a lighted table near the pool, and now and then, a pair would wander off toward the beach, arms entwined.

"I may as well go along, too. I've got a couple of chapters to finish tonight, and I brought along three more books."

"I brought five."

"Mysteries?" He took her arm to steer her around the bridge table and forgot to release it.

She wasn't about to tell him they were romances. To each his own fantasy. His was a solution to every crime; hers, a happy ending for every couple. One was about as realistic as the other, but between the pages of a book, they were harmless enough.

"Uh-oh. Watch out for the Siamese twins," she murmured, seeing the honeymooners from 128D approaching.

Two could have passed easily on the walk between screened tennis courts and oleander hedge. Three could have scraped by. There was no way two joined couples could pass, and Gardiner didn't seem in any hurry to relinquish her arm. Which she'd allowed him to keep only because there were so many dark shadowy areas along the way, Daisy told herself.

"Buenas noches," he murmured politely, stepping back against the high screen at the last moment and pulling her against his chest.

Daisy felt the air rush from her lungs and told herself to watch it. Fruity drinks, palm trees, tropical flowers and moonlit waters were all very well in travel brochures. In real life they could be hazardous to your health.

Her eyelids drifted shut just for an instant, and immediately her traitorous senses took over. At a distance, the sound of music was overlaid by the whisper of surf against coral sands. The tantalizing fragrance of a thousand night blossoms was spiked by a deeper note—a musky masculine essence that was playing havoc with her hormones.

His chest was hard against her back—hard and warm. Her buttocks curved neatly into an area delineated by his flat abdomen and a pair of muscular thighs, and—

Oh, God!

Had she once imagined how his hands would feel on her body? The fantasy was nothing compared to the reality! Hard—they felt hard and warm and dry. She could feel the pressure of each individual finger through her silk sleeves—and the pressure was not easing, although the Siamese twins were long gone.

"Gardiner," she wheezed.

His body behind hers was rock hard. Everywhere. She thought she heard him swear, but just then the band wound up its version of "Girl from Ipanema" and the crowd roared its approval.

Or was the roaring her own pulses? "Gardiner, wake up!"

"Oh. Yeah. I, uh... the m-m-moon. I was waiting t-t-to see if the moon was going to r-r-rise over the wall."

"Not unless the earth suddenly tilted on its axis while I wasn't looking," Daisy said dryly, extricating herself from his hands. She hadn't a clue where the moon was, or which direction they were facing, but it was the sort of remark Daisy Valentine would make. And she'd better get herself back into her role before someone discovered what a fake she was.

* * *

Gardiner took his book with him to breakfast the next morning, and was chagrined to find that Daisy had brought one along, as well. Not her own, though. This was one he recognized from the hotel's so-called library, which consisted of whatever paperbacks had been left behind by previous guests. His slightly amused look didn't go unnoticed.

"You like spy thrillers?"

"Oh, well . . . this one's a bit dated, but I never got around to reading it."

"You want to do the fruit while I do the eggs?"

Breakfast was buffet-style, with a fruit bar on one side and a grill on the other. They agreed on who wanted what and spilt up, rejoining a few minutes later at the table.

It was crowded again, and there was a fresh cadre of waiters on duty. Daisy beckoned to one and said, *"Mantequeso, por favor."*

The boy looked at her blankly and she repeated it. And then repeated it again.

"Try *mantequilla,*" Gardiner suggested quietly, and the waiter scurried away, looking relieved.

"Are you sure it's not *mantequeso?* I could have sworn . . ."

Gardiner assured her it wasn't and then tried to salve her ego. *"Queso*—cheese. It's another milk product. Logical mistake."

"I didn't really want butter, anyway," she mumbled, biting off a big chunk of the hard dry bread that accompanied every meal.

The butter arrived, and Gardiner spread her bread with it. He wasn't exactly grinning, but the effect was the same. Daisy shoved her Mexican-style scrambled eggs around her plate and fumed. How the devil could she maintain her attitude when she kept making a fool of herself? With an audience yet!

"There's a native village several kilometers from here. Would you like to try for a couple of adult-sized bikes and go exploring?"

Daisy still hadn't figured out the kilometer business. Was it larger or smaller than a mile? Why hadn't she been given the kind of brain that dealt in hard facts instead of a head full of *queso* that was good only for formulating the occasional hazy concept?

"I've made other plans, thanks," she said, pushing back her chair.

Several hours later, having washed all the underwear that had accumulated during the rainy spell and draped it over the arms and back of a sunny lawn chair, Daisy was sitting out behind her room on the five square feet of private patio alloted her, surrounded by the morning's plunder, when Gardiner strolled through the privacy wall of oleander that separated one unit from another.

"Fancy meeting you here," he remarked, eyes warming to pewter as he surveyed her morning wash. "So this is what your backyard looks like."

Startled, she was immediately on the defensive. "So?"

"So how was your outing?" So she wore peach-colored stuff underneath, he mused. With lace. He tried to visualize her in it and succeeded too well for comfort.

"My outing?"

Expediently shifting his position, Gardiner propped one foot on the low edge of her deck. He knew damned well she'd gone haring off down the beach by herself right after breakfast. He'd watched her go, just as he had sat out on his balcony and watched for her to come back. All in all, he was feeling pretty pleased with himself. The old Gard Gentry would have backed off at the first sign of discouragement.

Hell, the old Gardiner would never have risked trying anything with a woman as glossy as Daisy Valentine in the first place. But the new Gardiner would.

What's more, the new Gardiner had a feeling this tall haughty beauty wasn't half as glossy as she wanted the world to believe. There were cracks in her patina you could drive a coal car through.

He picked up a piece of the bleached coral she'd been spreading around her. "Hmm…nice pattern. Have you seen Chichen Itza yet?"

It took her a moment to catch up. She'd been staring at his hands while he fingered her coral. "Uh, no. Not yet."

"Well worth seeing."

"I'm sure," she said noncommittally.

"Aquaria?"

"I beg your pardon?"

He gave her credit—she was trying hard, but it wasn't going to do her any good. He had her on the run, and he wasn't going to let up, not until he'd routed her out of her shell. Puzzles had always intrigued Gard Gentry, which was why he'd been drawn to the world of mathematics in the first place. There was usually an answer if you dug deep enough, tried hard enough and long enough.

Who was this woman who hacked off her hair in a style that not one woman in a thousand could get away with—and left the gray strands to shine through? Who wore fire-engine-red lipstick but didn't bother to mask the fine lines around her eyes and across her forehead? Who dressed one day like a model in one of those fancy fashion magazines Georgia was so fond of, and the next wore a matched set of garbage bags?

And right now, sitting in front of a chair full of wet socks and lacy underwear, she was staring him down with a pair of back-off-buddy eyes. Dark eyes. Not anthracite dark, but bituminous dark—soft, with warm undertones when she smiled.

Which was damned seldom.

Gardiner had always liked puzzles. But a few rare puzzles, human and otherwise, didn't have a conclusive solution. They simply lured a man in deeper and deeper, so that he couldn't back out if his life depended on it. Like one of the endless underground caves he'd risked his neck in as a boy.

"All these rocks." He tossed up a broken chunk of brain coral and caught it, never taking his eyes from her face. "I've seen people with big salt-water aquaria fill the tanks with this kind of stuff. Probably has an effect on the pH, though—I'd check it out with an expert before I put it in with your fish."

Daisy curled her legs around her hips in a pose more graceful than the spraddle-legged one she'd been caught in. "*If* I had a fish tank, and *if* I intended to use these in it, I assure you I would consult an expert first. But I don't, and I'm not, so I won't."

"Right," he said with a grin.

"Right!"

"You any good at sailboarding?"

How could anything that looked so effortless from a distance be so damned difficult in actual practice? They had waited until the beach was deserted, until everyone else had gone in to shower and dress for dinner. The colorful sailboards were racked up on the beach, and Gardiner stopped by the shack to check out a couple.

"Need instructions?" the concessionaire asked. "I can schedule you and the lady for tomorrow morning about ten."

"No thanks, we've been watching. We'll just get the feel of it today—there's not enough wind to get into too much trouble."

"Yeah, man—whatever you say." The chocolate-colored youth with the bleached-blond hair lifted an eyebrow toward where Daisy waited, and grinned.

Gardiner's jaw thrust out as he stalked off. Having traded their membership cards and room keys for beach towels and the privilege of using the boards, he decided he didn't like the fellow's attitude. He was a jerk. What's more, if he didn't keep his eyes on his own affairs and off Daisy's body, he'd wind up wearing a pair of beefsteaks instead of those Foster Grants.

What the hell's gotten into you, buddy? You're reverting to type. Old man Gimp Gentry's oldest kid, ready to duke it out, huh?

God, it had been a long time since he'd felt the adrenaline racing through him that way. He grinned. It felt kind of good. A man could go stale, shut up in classrooms for years at a time with only the occasional library date to break the monotony.

Daisy broke into his thoughts. "What are you laughing at? For all you know I'm terrific at this."

He tried valiantly not to stare at the length of golden tanned leg exposed to the coral rays of the setting sun. Tried and failed. "Feel like making a small wager?"

"On what?" She tugged down the legs of her suit.

Why the dickens couldn't she wear a bikini? That plain black conservatively cut thing she had on was having a wicked effect on his blood pressure. "Uh, falls? Say the best two out of three?"

"Confident, aren't we?"

He wanted to reach out and touch the crow's feet at the corners of her laughing eyes. He wanted to touch her all over. A little desperately, he picked up one of the boards and headed for the water.

Twenty minutes later, they were both laughing helplessly, having failed repeatedly to maintain a vertical position for more than thirty seconds at a time. "Where did you say you got all that athletic skill of yours?" Daisy gasped, raking her dripping bangs off her forehead.

"What, you don't believe me? I was a star quarterback, lady. To this day my name is on three plaques and two loving cups in a certain high-school gym in West Virginia!"

They were wading ashore, towing the boards behind them. "Funny—you don't look like a star quarterback." She forced herself not to stare at the glittering drops of water that hung from every curl on his chest and thighs. He was beautifully constructed.

He shrugged. "I came along before steroids hit the boonies. What about you?"

"What about me?" Startled, she looked down at her own chest, and was chagrined to see that her nipples were standing out in bold relief against the low plateau of her bosom. She had come along before silicone hit the boonies, too—not that she'd have had the nerve. With her luck, a breast transplant would have ended up settling somewhere around her hips. "Was I a jock, you mean?"

"Let me guess—track?"

"Nope."

They reached shore and bent to lift the boards, carrying them back to the open storage facility. Gardiner grabbed both towels and tossed her one. "Basketball?"

"Two left feet."

"You had to have done something. Give me a clue, huh?"

Daisy wiped at her hair and then her face and slung the towel over her chest. A drop of water slipped off a point of hair and trickled down the side of her face. Catching it with her finger, she thought for a moment. "Okay. Manual dexterity."

In the afterglow of the setting sun, she was coral and copper, amber and gold. Her bathing suit was hugging her body the way he'd like to, and Gardiner inhaled deeply and blew out a lungful of air through his teeth. "Hmm...manual dexterity."

She grinned, totally unself-conscious. Her lipstick was gone, and her hair, where she'd shoved it back, was standing on end. She was the most beautiful thing he'd ever seen in all of his forty-one deprived years.

He reached out with his towel and blotted her left cheek. And then her right one. "Manual dexterity,

hmm?'' And then he looped the towel around the back
of her head and gave it a sharp tug, so that she fell
against him. "Got it—you were a juggler, right?"

She giggled into his neck. Her hands shoved at his
chest, but he was wet and so were her hands, and they
slid off and somehow ended up clutching his waist.
When she tried to lean back, he let her go only far
enough for his own purposes . . . and his own purposes
had been building all afternoon. All day. All the past
week, in fact.

The first touch of her lips carried enough voltage to
light up the eastern seaboard. Stunned, Gardiner
opened his eyes. Hers were shut tight. For a single
nanosecond he considered backing out while he still
possessed the willpower. Then he shut his eyes again
and got down to the business of kissing her out of his
system.

Daisy felt the last glimmer of common sense flicker
and die, and she opened her mouth to the tentative
thrust of his tongue. God, he was intoxicating!

*Stop it right this minute, Daisy Valentine! You'll be
sorry! You know where this kind of thing can lead!*

She wrapped her arms more securely around his
waist and thrust back timidly. And then more boldly.
She'd worry about it tomorrow.

Four

———

The first thing that entered Gardiner's head when he was rational enough to think again was that he'd been right about her. Buried under all that high-gloss polish was a warm and sensuous woman just waiting to be set free.

The second thing that entered his head was that he was the last man on earth to even think of getting involved. What could he do for her?

What could she do for him?

Deliberately closing his mind to reason, he tossed the beach towel onto the sand and urged her down, kneeling beside her. At that moment, he could no more have walked away from her than he could have hopped on a sailboard and skimmed across the channel to Cozumel.

"It's getting dark," Daisy murmured. She was on her back, her features delineated by the last red glow of sunset.

"Yeah," he whispered. Leaning over, he stared down at her, wondering what made her so different from all other women he had met—and so appealing. "You're not cold, are you?" Crazy question. Her skin was hot to the touch, like sun-warmed silk.

"Oh, no. Are you?"

Instead of answering, he lowered himself so that his chest was just brushing hers. Simple body heat exploded into raw flames. "I guess I'm not too good at this sort of thing," he said shakily.

Daisy let her hands trail over his shoulders, down the smooth swell of his biceps. He smelled clean, salty, masculine. It was either Caribbean voodoo or some bewitching mathematical formula, she decided, because normally she was the most sensible of women. Normally, she wouldn't be caught dead in a situation like this. "I'm a bit out of practice, too," she confided, trying for blasé and missing it by a mile. "It's not as if either of us was the type to..."

"To get involved?"

"To get involved," she echoed absently. One of his legs had slid over hers, and his toe was rubbing against the sandy sole of her foot. "That tickles," she whispered.

"Tickles, hmm?" He did it again, slower, and with cataclysmic results.

Gardiner tried to back off, but it was as if some nameless force was pressing him down, down, down. He wanted to touch her all over. He wanted to absorb her. He wanted to become one with her in the most basic way—and in ways he had never even dreamed of before.

"Hot chills," Daisy gasped, shuddering, and her soft laughter tantalized his ear. Lifting himself up onto his elbows, he captured her face between his hands and gazed down at her in the near darkness.

"What about this?" he whispered. His mouth covered hers just as his hand slid down to cover her breast. Brushing her lips with a gentleness that strained the boundaries of his control, he shut off any possible protest she might have made. The kiss was dangerously intimate, incredibly tender—yet it was only a meeting of moist lips, seasoned lightly with salt and sand.

Daisy began to melt inside. She was still thinking, *I'll put an end to this before it goes any further* when the last shred of reason she possessed dissipated like fog under a blazing sun. Gardiner's lips parted hers just the least bit more and began to move slowly, testing texture, taste and shape. Long before she felt the first plunge of his tongue, she was whimpering with need. As if it were the signal he'd been waiting for, he shifted his hips until he was pressing her into the sand, letting her know of his own growing need. Before either of them could stop it, the kiss escalated until they were both wild with wanting.

Abruptly, Gardiner rolled over onto his back, taking her with him. He fumbled at her straps, tugging them down as far as her upper arms, where they clung, trapped by the weight of her body on his.

"I warned you I wasn't very good at this," he said with a short laugh that sounded as if he were hurting.

"I don't know what you call good, exactly," Daisy began, and then shut up, because her own voice was every bit as unreliable as his.

"Uh, smooth? There's probably a graceful way to disrobe you, but..."

Daisy let her forehead drop against his collarbone and willed herself not to roll her hips against him. But oh, Lord, how she wanted to! The urge was almost overpowering! "Thank goodness at least one of us has enough common sense not to try and disrobe on a public beach." She even managed a small chuckle, which didn't help matters between them one bit.

Gardiner groaned and tilted his pelvis slightly. Daisy closed her eyes and curled her fists in the heated shelter of his armpits. Together they lay like that until their breathing came under control. Daisy grew gradually aware of the contrast between the chill evening air on her naked back and fiery heat generated where their two bodies touched. Which was everywhere that counted.

With only two thin scraps of nylon between them—his and hers—the power of his masculinity was unmistakable.

"This wasn't very smart," she said with a sigh. Unthinking, she touched the tip of her tongue to the skin of his neck, savoring the saltiness, the heat, the unique flavor that was Gardiner Gentry. Smart! God, it was the stupidest thing she'd done since that day ten years ago when she'd impulsively agreed to drive to South Carolina and marry a gorgeous, vain, ambitious law student who was seven years her junior!

"Wanna wash off the sand?" Gardiner asked, his voice reminding her of coffee grounds—dark, rich and gritty. One of his hands had been scouring her back, moving in slow circles, for a long time. She hadn't stopped him because she'd hoped the counterirritant might have helped.

It hadn't. "It's either that or the cleaning crew will have to trade in their vacuum cleaner for a backhoe."

"Remember those guys who sleep on a bed of nails?"

"You mean fakirs? It couldn't be much worse than sandy sheets."

"How about cracker crumbs?"

"Only if they're very, *very* stale."

Neither of them made a move to get up. Daisy because she couldn't summon the energy, and Gardiner, she thought with amusement, because he was buried under a hundred and twenty-two pounds of sandy wet woman. "I don't see a chain hoist around here. How about I roll off and you help me up?" she bargained.

"Deal. But watch where you plant those knees and elbows, okay?"

So much for the flames of passion. Like most other flames, they were easily quenched by a little sand and salt water. Plus a healthy dose of common sense. Still, for a while there, Daisy reminded herself, it had been a near thing.

Warily, they rinsed off in the surf, taking care not to touch.

Silently, Gardiner walked her to her room.

Courteously, he waited until she'd let herself inside.

Cursing impotently under his breath, he turned toward the stairs that led up to his own floor. He told himself he'd better back off before he got in over his head.

"Make that retroactive," he muttered, stabbing his key into the lock.

There were plenty of scheduled activities on tap. Gardiner scanned the list, selected a few that would carry him through his remaining week. He took to skipping breakfast, grabbing a burger at the bar for lunch, and waiting for the last half hour to eat dinner. She ate early.

On the rare times when they happened to meet, both were defensive. Both were wary, which only made them increasingly aware. He refused to admit that he missed her. She wasn't his type.

Not that he had a type. But if he had, she wouldn't be it. She was too glitzy. Too outspoken.

Yeah, and that was another thing he missed about her—that dry wit. Those outrageous remarks she came out with at the most unexpected times. He'd come to suspect that they were a part of some carefully constructed defense system, but that didn't make them any less effective.

Oh, he still saw her, of course. Getting into a cab one afternoon. Perched on top of a roadside ruin within bicycling distance of the hotel, her paints spread around her and that stupid hat pulled down over her brow. Practicing her shaky Spanish on the cleaning crew.

Turning in the paperback she'd borrowed from the office.

Lingering outside, Gardiner noticed that she didn't take down a replacement off the shelf. A streak of unfamiliar perversity made him hang around until she came outside. "How'd you like it?"

She caught her breath, but recovered quickly. "How did I like what? Oh—the book? Pretty good."

"If you couldn't find anything you liked in there, you're welcome to look over my stock—I'm through with the lot." And before she could take it or leave it, he added, "But you probably don't care for mysteries."

Daisy bridled. There was no other word to describe it. "I like mysteries just fine," she said coolly. "As it happens, I haven't finished all the books I brought to read."

"If you've got even a few you're done with, I could use some fresh reading material. The establishment's stock is pretty pathetic."

Great. Just wonderful. And when he discovered that the books she had were all romance novels she could just imagine his reaction. Never mind that the stories were every bit as well written, not to mention filled with just as much tension and adventure as any other genre. "I, uh ... I haven't quite finished yet."

"With *any* of them?"

There was that Central American jungle story. The ever exciting soldier-of-fortune-hired-to-bring-out-the-daughter-of-an-American-diplomat theme. If she stripped off the covers, he might not recognize it as a romance until he was too involved to put it down. It would serve him right if he unknowingly read it and loved it!

"Well, there is one, but it's in pretty sad shape," she said. "If you'll wait right here, I'll get it for you."

"I can come get it."

Daisy flung back her head and looked down her nose at him—which took a bit of doing, as he was about three inches taller than she was. "I said I'll get it," she enunciated carefully, and he nodded and moved over to a wooden poolside chair.

Regretfully, she stripped every page of incriminating evidence from her book and called herself a hypocrite. What difference did it make what he thought of her reading material? She didn't think all that much of his, for that matter. Anyone who could derive entertainment from reading about violent death and dismemberment had to be a bit warped.

At least in her book, the positive values outweighed the negative. The hero wasn't the guy who could devise the most diabolical method for dispatching his victims and getting away with it. Or even the harddrinking, hard-fighting jerk who eventually brought his slightly less legal counterpart to justice.

Scowling, she glared at her image in the mirror. A few minutes later, her nose de-shined, her eyebrows brushed and her lipstick freshened, she sprayed a cloud of eau de cologne in the air and walked through it. Then she snatched up her mutilated book and stalked out, slamming the door behind her.

She didn't see him all the rest of the day. She had pretended an urgent errand and dashed off after handing over the book, and then she'd spent the day moping around just out of sight of the hotel on a stretch of beach so rugged and forbidding that no one ever went there.

At first it had suited her just fine. She'd unpacked her paints, but there had been too much scenery, bringing on a sensory overload. She'd dozed for a while, and then opened the book she had brought along, only to find the sun too glaring to read with any degree of comfort. By then she was getting hungrier by the minute, but she'd refused to give in and go back.

The bottle of distilled water she'd bought at the store was tepid and tasteless, and the package of crackers she'd bought to go with it were disgustingly stale.

Raisins. She would give five dollars for a box of raisins.

Stretching out on her rocky perch, she sighed. She was really too miserable to linger much longer, but she didn't want to go back. Not yet, at least.

Bird-watching was fine as far as it went, but after the first couple of hours, even that got boring. Especially as she didn't know the names of most of the birds she saw. Crows, bluejays, cardinals and robins—those she could identify. She couldn't even guess at their Mexican counterparts.

There were some lovely wildflowers, equally nameless, just a few yards into the bush, but she kept remembering what Gardiner had said about poisonous reptiles. For all she knew, the flowers could be poisonous, too. Some plants were. All she needed to make her stay complete was an itchy oozy case of poison ivy.

Great. She was too chicken to explore the countryside, too chicken to hang around the hotel and risk running into Gardiner, and afraid to swim alone without a lifeguard in attendance. "Here we have it, folks— the all new, completely self-sufficient Daisy Valentine!"

What a crock.

By the time Daisy realized that her new sunscreen was not exactly sweat-proof, it was too late. Every inch of exposed skin—which included a considerable area, thanks to her relative privacy—was the exact same color as the bougainvillea that spilled over the walls back at the hotel. Bright pink.

"A zillion pesos a day for a cool comfortable room," she muttered, "and I sit out here sulking on a miserable rock until I'm parboiled. While other people are dining on conch seviche and grilled tenderloin under a battery of ceiling fans, I'm sprawled out here on a hot lumpy rock, stuffing myself on lukewarm artificial water and limp crackers. Real smart, Valentine. Real smart."

It was too early for dinner, too late for lunch, and she was starving. Five days from now, she would go back home after her glamorous Caribbean vacation, peeling like a new potato, and all because of a man who didn't even know how to dress for a darned beach resort! Gray chinos, gray deck shoes, khakis and white shirts. Was that any way to dress in a place like this? He didn't even possess a rude T-shirt or a pair of shark-bait-neon swim trunks, much less a Mexican *guyaberra!*

Face it—the man was a jerk, and she was a jerkess for even noticing him, much less . . .

Much less . . .

Gardiner noticed her right off. She was wearing coral tonight. All over. Except for her feet, which were encased in thick white socks and yellow sandals. He didn't know a whole lot about fashion—slightly less than the average groundhog knew, actually—but something didn't seem quite right about the way she looked, even to him.

Tonight her hat was pulled down until it nearly covered her face. She usually left it off after sunset. And for once, she wasn't wearing hubcaps in her ears. It had gotten to the point where he looked forward to seeing what outrageous stuff she would attach to her body next. Rocks tied down with brass chains, cages of wooden birds, papier-mâché painted every color of the rainbow and stuck full of fake gemstones. The crazy thing was that, on her, they looked good. Looked great, in fact.

He sighed and stood up at the table for two in the corner. There was nothing smaller, otherwise he'd have asked for it. And the place was jammed, another busload having just arrived from the airport.

The maître d' brought her over. Having been there for more than a week, they were considered almost family by now. *"Buenas noches, señor, señorita,"* he crooned as he held out her chair.

Scowling, Daisy muttered a response and then tacked on a *gracias*.

"I didn't want to be here, you know," she told him the instant the young man moved away.

Gardiner shrugged. "Pretend you're alone. I will." He'd just been seated after a wait of some twenty minutes, and hadn't even had time to go look over the buffet yet. And he damned well wasn't going to skip dinner just to please her.

Daisy took a deep breath, stared down at her napkin and felt her eyes sting with tears. If she weren't so hungry, she'd leave. On the other hand, why should she? She had paid for her meals, the same as he had. Why should she miss anything just because some bony-faced college professor with stainless-steel eyes kept getting in her way wherever she turned?

Without excusing himself, he left the table, and Daisy felt her chin actually tremble. She hadn't cried in years. It simply wasn't something she did—especially for no good reason at all. PMS, probably. Only it wasn't time for it. Besides, she always got bitchy, not weepy. She might gripe and snap and drop things, but she had never been known to get teary over rugged unhandsome faces and strong accommodating shoulders, and wide hands that looked so hard, but could be so gentle....

Uttering a rude word under her breath, Daisy raked back her chair and stalked up to the salad bar, where she piled a large plate with some of everything, whether or not she liked it. Whether or not she even recognized it.

Gardiner lifted an acrobatic eyebrow, but didn't say a word as she doggedly worked her way through fish salad, bean salad, coleslaw, tossed salad, cheeses, papaya, jicama, watermelon, pineapple and something that looked cool and tomatoey, with lots of little green things mixed in with it.

Strangling, she dropped her fork and snatched up her water glass. Tears filled her eyes and overflowed.

Quietly, Gardiner signaled a waiter and asked for a glass of *leche*. Daisy wanted to ask for a fire extinguisher, but Berlitz probably didn't cover it, even if she could catch her breath.

Someone placed a glass of milk in front of her, and Gardiner said, "Drink it."

Desperate, she did.

"Next time, don't be so damned greedy."

"I beg your pardon?"

"And if you beg my pardon one more time," he said calmly, "I'm going to touch you where it'll hurt the most. How old are you, anyway? Thirteen? Ten?"

She drew herself up stiffly—no great task, since she didn't dare let her back touch the slats on the chair. "It's none of your business how old I am, and you may keep your snide remarks to yourself. I don't find them particularly amusing." She blotted her wet cheeks with as much dignity as she could muster.

His face was unreadable. Not that she was interested in reading it.

Oh, damn. Her mouth was better—the milk had helped, when the water hadn't done a thing. But her eyes were still watering, and by now, her mascara had probably melted, which made everything worse, for reasons she didn't even want to think about. Her whole vacation was screwed up, and she hadn't the slightest idea why—she only knew it had something to do with the man seated across the table from her, calmly eating his squid on rice.

"Want me to get you some dessert? Your blood sugar's probably out of kilter from all that sun."

She latched on to the excuse. "Does that happen?"

"Hell, I don't know. A bad burn—I figure it's something like shock, and people use sweets for shock, don't they?"

"I think they use smelling salts," Daisy replied, glad to hear that her voice was reasonably steady, no matter that she felt as wobbly as a day-old kitten.

He brought her an assortment. Daisy started with the flan and worked her way through two kinds of cake, finishing up with the fruit gelatin. Stress always affected her appetite.

"You're not afraid of putting on weight, are you?" Gardiner asked after she'd demolished the lot. He signaled for coffee and waited until it had been poured. "Most women I know steer clear of desserts."

Daisy actually smiled at him while she laced her coffee with generous portions of cream and sugar. She felt much better. Food always did that for her. "It's the Valentine metabolism," she told him. "My grandfather heaped his plate three times a day and came back for seconds, and he was tall and skinny as a rail until the day he died."

"What did he do for a living? Lumberjack?"

"Hardly. He was a tobacco auctioneer during the season, he ran a sawmill in the off-season, and raised mules on the side for fun and profit—mostly fun."

They drank their coffee in companionable silence for several minutes, until the people at the next table got up to leave. One of the women had looped her large bamboo-frame purse over the back of her chair, and in freeing it, she accidentally raked it over Daisy's shoulders.

Eyes closed in agony, Daisy leaned forward and drew her breath between clenched teeth.

"That bad, huh?"

Wordlessly, she nodded. Her shoulders had caught the brunt of the sun. In deference to a patch of tall grass she'd had to cross to get to the spit of land she sought, she had worn slacks going and coming. She'd worn her hat most of the time. But clothes were hot, and she'd soon peeled them off and slathered on another coat of sunscreen, for all the good it had done her.

Neither hat nor sunscreen had protected her against the heavy sweat-inducing humidity, frequent splashes in the shallow cooling water, and a fierce reflected sun.

Gardiner waited until they were outside to make his offer. "I've got a bottle of some pretty good stuff in my room."

Daisy's eyes widened. "Thanks, but I think I'll skip it tonight. I have a soda wrapped in wet towels sitting outside on my patio keeping cold. I hope." One of the hotel's less endearing quirks, along with the nonstop canned music and the lack of telephones, was the lack of an ice machine. It bothered her less than the music did, considerably more than the lack of a phone.

"Uh, not that kind of bottle. Something for your sunburn. Or maybe you've got it covered?"

She shook her head. "I hadn't planned on getting burned. I always use sunscreen."

"*Qué pasa?*"

She shrugged and then winced as tender skin wrinkled painfully.

"The label on my new bottle was written in Spanish. How was I to know it wasn't waterproof?"

They were moving in the direction of their units, as if by mutual consent. It was early yet—ordinarily, they would have lingered at one of the tables beside the pool, either separately or together.

Gardiner saw her to her door and said, "I'll bring it down. Can't guarantee it, as I haven't had to use it yet."

Every instinct she possessed warned Daisy that it was a mistake to agree. *Tell him no thanks and good night, goofus.*

But I'm hurting, darn it!

You could end up hurting a lot more if you're not careful.

What could happen when I look like a boiled lobster, for goodness' sake? The man's not a sadist, he's a math teacher.

The two are not mutually exclusive. I'm warning you, Daisy Bell Valentine—

Butt out! Who asked you, anyway?

"Shall I come around to your back door so you won't have to let me in?" Gardiner asked. The hotel also had a lot going for it, one of the nicer things being that security was not a problem. The guests evidently had other things on their minds, and the staff was above reproach. For the sake of cross ventilation, Daisy always kept the patio door open, the screen giving her the illusion, at least, of privacy.

She nodded. Closing the front door, she leaned against it for a moment, wondering if too much sun could affect a person's brain.

An orderly man by nature, Gardiner knew exactly where the lotion was. Right between the insect repellant and the shaving cream. But orderly or not, by the time he closed his hands over the bottle, his shaving kit looked as if it had weathered a typhoon.

He took the stairs two at a time, swung around the corner and leapt over the low wall to the grass, whistling softly under his breath. Nearing her privacy wall, he slowed, raking his fingers through his hair, and schooled his face to show proper concern. The woman was suffering. No man with a conscience would allow her to suffer when he had the means at his disposal to bring her relief.

Remembering the last bad sunburn he'd had—he'd been about twenty at the time, and pretty damned invincible—he winced. Tonight was going to be hell on her poor scorched body. No matter how you worked it, there was no practical way to bring wrinkled sheets and tender flesh together without causing pain. And the sheets in this place were more utilitarian than luxurious.

Maybe a bottle of hootch wasn't a bad idea. If he'd had one. It wouldn't have hurt to take the edge off a little.

He whistled softly before he broke through the oleander, just to give her warning in case she was...

She wasn't. "Come in. Oh—Sooth Sun. I remember this. My mother used to use it on me. Thanks a lot, Gardiner."

If she thought she was getting rid of him that easily, she was in for an education. "Have you got something soft to sleep in that doesn't have a whole lot of seams?"

"My nightgown."

"Yeah, well... sure, that ought to do just fine." He was standing just inside her screen. She hadn't exactly invited him inside, but then, she hadn't told him to bug off, either. "Seams can be pretty miserable."

She nodded. In the incandescent light of the large airy room, she looked all one color. He didn't know if she had on lipstick or not—all he knew was that she was beautiful. In her sock feet, with her hair all spiky around her face, she was the loveliest thing he'd ever seen, and he had a funny feeling in the pit of his stomach that he was in more trouble than he'd been in since he'd got himself pinned down between a mine field and Cong sniper at Nha Trang, with his M-1 lying on the other side of a strip of punji sticks.

Five

—

"**W**hy don't I just wait out here on the back porch until you get ready?"

Daisy stepped back, eyes narrowed suspiciously. "Why don't you just hand over the bottle—naturally I expect to pay you for it—and go play checkers or something?"

"You baked your back, right?"

"So I'll sleep on my stomach."

"And that's another thing—do you have any talcum?" Gardiner stepped past her and glanced around.

Without saying a word, Daisy spun around, marched to her bath-dressing-room area, and returned a moment later with a can of baby powder. She held it out to him. "Take it. We'll trade." She wanted him out of her sight, and most especially out of her bedroom. He wasn't a huge man, but he took up an extraordinary amount of air for his size.

"Look, can we cut this short?" she said. "I'm not feeling particularly hospitable at the moment." She felt rotten. Her skin was too tight, she felt feverish, and every body part she possessed was throbbing painfully. Her feet were so swollen she'd probably have to cut her sandals off. She'd paid an outrageous amount of money for those yellow sandals—one more dumb thing she could credit her impulsiveness for. The list was growing faster than Pinocchio's nose.

Gardiner braced himself to stick it out. He knew damned well she didn't want him there, but she *needed* him! She needed *someone,* and he hadn't noticed her buddying up to any of the other guests. "I'm not asking for anything, Daisy, I'm offering. No, I'm insisting. You might need a doctor for all I know—" She tried to interrupt but he ploughed right on. "But there's none around, so I'm it, unless you want to call in one of the staff and ask them to smear that stuff on your back for you."

The staff was ninety-nine percent male. About three percent spoke English. Knowing Daisy—and surprisingly, Gardiner felt he knew her pretty well—she'd have to be raw, bleeding and broken before she'd ask a perfect stranger to do something so personal. "You need fluids. I'm going to go along and see how much fruit juice I can round up, and while I'm gone, why don't you get into your pajamas or whatever and get ready for bed. But first..."

Dumbfounded, Daisy watched as he flipped back the spread and top sheet on her king-size bed and sprinkled talcum powder over the entire surface. "There, that ought to ease the wrinkles. Something my grandma taught me when I used to slip away and go skinny-dipping the minute the river warmed up enough so I didn't freeze. Amazing how many body parts can get sunburned when a guy's floating downriver on an inner tube.''

It was only the mental image of a gray-eyed, jay-bird-naked kid tubing down the river that kept Daisy from throwing him out on his ear. And only her own growing misery that kept her from laughing aloud.

"Oh, Lord . . . Look, go get me something to drink and I'll let you spread that stuff on my shoulders, all right?''

Not until he'd left did it occur to her that she had sounded almost as if she were granting him a favor. Groaning, she drew the curtains and began to get ready for bed. Even brushing her teeth hurt. At least it hurt when she opened wide enough to do it.

A frank assessment in front of the mirror a few minutes later brought on another groan. If she'd even suspected he had ulterior motives for wanting to get his hands on her body, one look was enough to dispel them. Her eyes, dark brown and normally slightly slanted, were now positively squinty, set as they were in the pale reverse-racoon goggles left by her sunglasses.

It was bad enough to know she looked grotesque. It was even worse to be utterly miserable along with it. Her short batiste gown, with its eyelet-embroidered neckline and hem, felt like burlap brushing against her tortured skin. As if that weren't depressing enough, her ankle bones seemed to have disappeared altogether.

"Oh, God, how could I have been so stupid?" It was a rhetorical question. More to the point, when was she going to smarten up?

"Daisy? You decent? I've brought three kinds of juice and some cold drinks."

"No, I'm not decent—I doubt if I'll ever be decent again, but I'm covered at least. Come on in, and if you say one word, I'll crown you with a coconut." She emerged from the bathroom, lotion in hand, in time to see Gardiner pawing his way through the draperies that covered the sliding patio doors. "Let me anoint my front first, and then I'll lie down and cover up and you can do my back. If you don't mind."

While Daisy smoothed the soothing blend of aloe and menthol over her legs from thigh to toe, sighing at the blessedly cool relief, Gardiner found a couple of glasses and poured them both some tomato juice. She sipped gratefully, wondering if he'd noticed that the color of her skin matched it exactly.

"Why don't you get in bed and pull your gown off now?"

There was no possible way she could read anything untoward in his suggestion. No man could be that desperate. The thought made her feel vaguely weepy again, but she dutifully set her glass aside and crawled under the sheet.

"I'll rinse these glasses out while you get ready," he said, and tactfully disappeared while she wrestled to remove the gown she'd just put on without chafing her tender skin. Then she rolled onto her stomach.

The powder had been a good idea. It was probably sticking to her lotiony legs, but she was beginning to feel slightly better. Part of it—a large part, perhaps—

was the feeling of being coddled. The last time she'd been coddled had been when she'd woken up with a face full of poison ivy on the morning of her ninth birthday party. Her eyes had swollen up until she'd looked like a bullfrog, and she had refused to let anyone see her. While she'd stayed in bed with a pillowcase over her head, her family and classmates had gone ahead with the party without her, singing "Happy Birthday" outside her bedroom window.

She had cried, which had washed off all the calamine lotion.

The mattress creaked beside her, and she felt a glow of body heat. It felt good. Suddenly she was so cold her teeth were chattering.

Gardiner's hand came down on her naked back with a palmful of icy lotion, and she yelped and reared up on her elbows. "Do you have to be so *rough?*"

"Sorry. I'd forgotten how cold that can feel. The worst is over, though, so lie down now and let me take care of you. Lady, you really did a job on yourself."

Soon every sensory nerve in her body zeroed in on her back as his hand began a slow circular motion. Pain ebbed away as if by magic. She was neither hot nor cold. The bed disappeared beneath her and she hung suspended somewhere in space, subject only to the balm of those wonderful healing hands.

She must have moaned. Her forehead rested on her arms, and her legs under the sheet were apart, not touching each other. Do-o-ownnn he went, using both hands, to the place just above her waist where her bathing suit had covered her, his fingers meeting at her spine. Then u-u-uppp again, into her hairline, forefingers curling around to touch the backs of her ears, and do-o-ownnn her neck, over her shoulders, out to her elbows and back again, and then down her sides, so cool, so smooth, so wonderful.

"B-b-better?" His touch was incredibly gentle, yet there was more than a hint of tension in his voice.

It should have hurt. The pressure alone should have been agony. Instead, Daisy felt a wonderful warm *something* uncoiling inside her that eclipsed every other sensation.

It wasn't that she was getting turned on—under the circumstances, that would have been too absurd for words. Besides, she'd always been notoriously difficult to arouse—as Beau had let her know on more than one occasion.

But it was *so* nice to be touched this way. "Promise me you won't ever stop," she murmured. The bed creaked as his weight shifted, and she felt something brush the back of her head. If she didn't know better, she might have thought it was his lips.

The bed creaked again and the hands moved on, hypnotically—grazing the sides of her breasts, never lingering there. It occurred to Daisy that lying on her stomach too long was having an effect on her breathing.

"Want something else to drink?"

"Mmm-hmm," she answered drowsily.

"More tomato juice?"

"S'prise me."

The hands moved down to the center of her back and lifted away, and she thought she heard him sigh unsteadily. Or maybe it had been her sigh. Whoever it was seemed to be shivering—and come to think of it, she was.

"Do you suppose I could possibly have some hot coffee?" she asked, carefully holding the sheet around her as she rolled over and sat up. "I know it's a lot to ask, but—"

"No problem. You might want to do your face and neck and the front of your, ah, back."

Fighting lethargy, Daisy anointed the areas mentioned while Gardiner went after coffee. She hoped he would remember how she liked hers. If not, she'd drink it black and pretend to like it. For someone who hated to be beholden to anyone, she was getting pretty heavily into debt.

There must be some way she could make it up to him. Maybe she could find something in the shop to send him—they had a few things for men. Bolos, belt buckles—some really neat hematite and sterling cuff links.

No. Not jewelry. It was too much, and besides, he'd probably hate it. A book. She would look for the latest mystery or spy novel and mail it to his college office.

Had he started on the book she'd lent him yet? Did he like it? Would he admit it if he did?

"Pint of cream and half a pound of sugar, right?" he asked, pushing his way through the curtains a few minutes later.

By then she'd put on her gown again and was sitting up in bed. There was a mirror on the opposite wall, into which she carefully avoided glancing. If she'd thought about it, she would have turned off half the lights in the room while she was up.

"Perfect," she said. "Gardiner, I don't know how to thank you. I've been so cranky, and you've gone out of your way to be helpful, and—"

He held up a hand and she stared at it. She could still feel his touch on her back, on the sides of her breasts. And as miserable as she was, misery wasn't at all the way to describe how she'd been feeling while he'd spread that wonderful gunk all over her sunburn.

"You did your face, too, didn't you?"

"I forgot it." Squinting up at his beautiful gray eyes and his handsome cheekbones and angular jaw, it occurred to her that she could easily forget which planet she was on.

"Look, I'll fix your coffee and pull up the bedspread—you'll probably get cool in the night. Then I'm going to take care of your face and get out of here so you can get some sleep, okay? I wish to hell we had room phones—or even two cans and a wet string. I'd hate to think you might need me in the night and I wouldn't know about it."

Daisy managed a weak chuckle. It was a measure of how much better she was feeling. Or how giddy. "I can't believe that's a bid to stay over, not with me looking like a boiled crab." *And I can't believe I just said that.* She took a deep breath and started over, trying for a modicum of dignity. "Thanks, Gardiner. I'll be just fine now. I might play vampire and hide out from the sun for a few days, so if you don't see me around, don't worry. And thanks again—for everything—if I don't happen to see you before you leave."

He stirred her coffee, placed it on her bedside table, and picked up the plastic bottle of sunburn lotion again. "Look up, hmmm?"

"I can do that."

"Let me," he said, and proceeded to stroke the stuff onto her forehead, her cheeks, her nose and her chin. She had shut her eyes instinctively, and wasn't prepared for the soft touch of his lips on hers.

It was over almost before it began. Much too soon—and not soon enough. By the time he had reached the door, she'd even begun to breathe again.

"See you tomorrow, Valentine."

Gardiner brought her breakfast. Under the circumstances, the dining-room staff let themselves be talked into making an exception to the no-room-service rule. Daisy opened the door promptly enough so that he didn't think he'd woken her up, but her rumpled gown attested to a restless night.

After one long look at the glow of pink flesh through white cotton lawn, he quickly raised his eyes. Hers were swollen almost shut, and she was in an understandably nasty mood. He handed over the tray along with one of his own undershirts—the sleeveless variety—brushed off her grudging thanks and pressed a finger to the tip of her nose, watching it turn white under the light pressure. Her lips, too, looked swollen. And smooth and soft and dangerously inviting.

"What's this for?" she muttered, glowering at the undershirt.

"Nightgown. I thought it might be softer than that ruffley thing you've got on."

"That wasn't necessary."

"Just shut up and take it, okay?" *It's ten o'clock in the morning, you creep! The woman's miserable, and all you can think about is jumping her bones!*

Embarrassed by his body's enthusiastic reaction, Gardiner leaned over to examine her swollen feet. "Whew, they look painful! You're really a mess, aren't you?"

"How gracious of you to notice," she grumbled. "I wish you weren't so damned decent so I could do a better job of hating you."

"Likewise, Blossom. Look, I'm taking off for the rest of the day. If you need anything, ask the cleaning crew—they'll fetch someone who speaks English. The word for help is *ayuda*."

Then he took himself off on a fishing trip with two couples—all teachers—from Dallas, just so he wouldn't hang around her door waiting for her to need him. And he went to a restaurant in Cancun with the same group later on that night for the same reason.

The next morning there was the jungle safari. Forcing himself not to think about how she might be faring on her own, Gardiner went along on the four-hour trek after signing up for another excursion that afternoon, rationalizing that it was his vacation, dammit. The honeymoon aspect had been virtually forgotten. What's more, he hadn't come all this way just to play nursemaid to some fool woman who'd been dumb enough to stay out in the sun too long!

But there was no denying the truth. Self-honesty was too ingrained a habit. And the truth was, he needed space. He needed perspective. The truth was, Gardiner Gentry was in serious danger of making a mistake he'd sworn never to repeat.

After a day and a half, Daisy had improved considerably. The liquid diet might have helped. She'd subsisted on all the juices and soft drinks Gardiner had supplied her with, plus the cookies and cheese she'd picked up at the store.

The first time she ventured out, it helped no end to discover that she wasn't the only one who had misjudged the power of the tropical sun. Or misread the label on a local product and bought a tan accelerator instead of a sunscreen.

"When did you get yours?" asked a parboiled blonde in an orange muumuu when Daisy tried to sneak up to the side of the bar and order a salad plate and limeade to go without being seen. Compared to the dining room, the bar served only the sketchiest of meals, but she wasn't yet ready for the hard slat-backed straight chairs and the curious eyes of some hundred-odd other diners. Haughty wasn't going to work for her when she looked like this.

"Monday," she said, surveying a face that was even redder than her own. "How about you?"

"Yesterday. We took one of the boat trips. Gawd, I hate to peel."

"I hate to hurt."

"My husband's been supplying me with iced tea. I literally bathe in the stuff."

"My...a friend of mine had some burn lotion. It took the fire out."

"Lucky you."

Yes, lucky her, Daisy thought dismally as she carried her plate and drink to the far corner of the Big Palapa and perched on the edge of one of the cold metal chairs. She was the sole resident—everyone else being either inside dining on the hotel's scrumptious buffet, out cavorting on the beach or bending an elbow at the thatched-roof bar.

"Go for it, Daisy," Cora Joan had said. "You work too darned hard, and you know what they say about all work and no play."

She'd gone for it. A vacation for one in an exotic tropical resort, with all the exotic tropical frills. If she spent one more hour staring at those exotic white stucco bedroom walls and counting those exotic red tiles on the floor, she'd go stark raving bonkers. Sunburn was bad. Terminal boredom was even worse.

Toying with the artistic arrangement of fruit, vegetables and cold meats on her plate, Daisy admitted that it wasn't boredom that had driven her out of her room. Nor even hunger.

She missed Gardiner. It wasn't like him to stay away for an entire day and a half.

On the other hand, maybe it was. What did she really know about the man? That he was originally from West Virginia? That he taught mathematics at a small college in Raleigh, North Carolina? That he was forty-one years old and had the kind of looks that could sneak up on a woman when she least expected it and knock her for a loop?

Oh, sure—he'd probably never be asked to grace the cover of *GQ*. She couldn't picture him in anything more flamboyant than gray, khaki or white. But he was kind, straightforward and a bit shy. He had a way of stammering when he got tense that made her want to gather him to her insignificant bosom and comfort him.

And herself.

One by one, Daisy dragged the peppers off to the edge of her plate and frowned at them. Shy. That was really underhanded of him, because a woman couldn't fight against a thing like that. If he'd come on to her like so many men had when she'd first been divorced, she could have handled him just fine. It hadn't taken her too long to figure out how effective a subzero drop-dead look could be. Delivered with just the right amount of indifference, it could flatten all but the most determined. And those she could usually outrun.

But Gardiner had used a different approach. In fact, she wasn't even sure it *was* an approach. If it was, then she'd better start revising her Star Wars plan, because he had come closer than any man ever had to slipping through her defenses.

And what she couldn't figure out was *why*. Was he trying to prove something? To add a little extra spice to his Mexican vacation?

Evidently his taste for spice had diminished. Or maybe he just didn't like easy game, she thought morosely as she absently crunched into one of the peppers she had so carefully raked aside.

Five more days, Daisy reminded herself a few hours later as she added another layer of Pomegranate Pink polish to her toenails. Five more days of no alarm clocks, no schedules, no appointments, no freezing rain, no traffic jams, no craftsmen calling in to whine about why they couldn't deliver the order they had been promising for six months, or why they had to have their money up front before they could buy supplies to even begin filling the order.

Five more days of balmy breezes, fantastic food cooked by someone else and cleaned up by someone else, five more days of daily maid service—not to mention five days of no telephone calls that invariably came at the most inconvenient time with a plea for funds for some worthy cause.

She sighed. Five more days before all possibility of seeing Gardiner Gentry again ended for good.

She shouldn't care. She *didn't* care, Daisy assured herself. All the same, she had more pride than to hang around the hotel on the off chance he might show up. There were plenty of things to do. Tours to take. Ruins to explore. Scenery to paint.

There were even a few other unattached women who had come in with the last group. Three real-estate brokers from Ontario and a corporate lawyer from Dallas. Interesting women, really... only she didn't have a whole lot in common with them.

Gardiner got in from fishing in time to see Daisy cross through the open area around the pool with the large black vinyl tote over her shoulder. There was a roll of paper and a bottle of water sticking out the top. Ten to one she was off on a painting trip.

He could catch her if he hurried....

Catch her and do what with her?

He knew what he'd like to do. He'd damned well like to march her right back to that king-size bed, peel off those orange shorts and that wild-looking shirt she was wearing on top and bury himself in her sweet flesh until he died there.

He let her go. Given any luck, he wouldn't see her again today, and then maybe he wouldn't dream about

her tonight. In no time at all, he'd be back to civilization, back to a third-floor apartment with a view of I-
40, back to classrooms that smelled of chalk and
sweeping compound, back to cafeteria food and
women who didn't remind him of things he was too old
to be dreaming about.

Six

Four days left. It had reached the point of being ludicrous. Daisy would wander outside, pretending to herself that she wasn't hoping for a glimpse of a familiar golden-brown head, a familiar bony face, a familiar set of broad shoulders, with hands planted just to the back of a pair of lean hips, legs spread slightly as if he were standing on the deck of a rolling ship.

Did he stand that way before a classroom? Was his school coed? Were all the girls in his classes in love with him? And if not, why not?

And then she'd catch sight of him. Brown eyes ranging over the crowd would suddenly collide with gray ones. Gray would slide away, quickly return, and then deliberately move away again.

Ludicrous, she told herself. A child's game.

But if it was only a child's game, then why did it leave her feeling so empty and incomplete?

Four days left, and she'd set herself a task. Visit the nearby native village she'd heard about, taking pictures if she could do it without imposing. Find a good shady vantage point far enough away so that she wouldn't feel self-conscious and spend the rest of the day painting.

She was determined to take something home with her besides a peeling nose, a bag full of beach debris and a bunch of unwelcome memories.

The assistant rec director had obliged her with instructions. He obviously thought she was crazy to even want to go there.

"Hey, it's only a bunch of grass shacks and a lot of pigs, chickens and *niños*—the place doesn't even have a name. You want picturesque? Why not get it from the window of the tour bus? We've got one leaving in twenty minutes bound for Cobá—I can sign you up right now, thirty bucks American. It'll take you right past a bunch of those places, with a stopoff at a souvenir shop run by the grandson of one of the original Mayan bigwigs, God knows how many generations removed."

He was obviously a real sensitive guy. Daisy suspected he was responsible for the constant barrage of canned music. He seemed the type.

"No thanks. I always get sick on buses."

He took a step backward as if it might be contagious, and she hurried on to grab a decent bike before the best ones were all taken.

It was one of those days made in heaven especially for travel-bureau photographers. Honeybees swarmed over the plentiful wildflowers. Intoxicating fragrances, laced with the mild salt tang of the nearby sea, filled her lungs. Her favorite peach-bellied birds swooped back and forth across the narrow trail in front of her as if leading the way, while smaller ones, equally colorful, equally anonymous, sang cheerfully in a language that needed no translation.

The rustling noises in the brush that closed in on both sides of the jungle trail didn't bother her at all. Nothing could threaten her on a day like this—it was heavenly. It would be even more heavenly if she'd had someone to share it with her.

She'd gone perhaps a mile and a half when the soft jungle rustlings suddenly increased in volume. Bigger birds? Probably. She'd seen some big black carnivorous-looking creatures perched in a dead tree some distance back. Much too large for songbirds. Too large even for crows. Even so, they were hardly large enough to pluck her off her bike and carry her off to their nests to feed their young.

She managed a nervous smile at the thought as the noises grew louder. Not that she was really frightened—all those Mayan jaguar carvings were hundreds of years old. Thousands, probably. Besides, everyone knew that cats didn't thrash through the jungle—they slunk. It was probably just an escaped pig. Cora Joan would get a kick out of hearing how she'd gone flying down a bumpy trail on a pink-and-orange bicycle, being chased by a pig.

She wasn't frightened—not really. But the faster she pedaled, the faster her hyperactive imagination churned out visions of saber-toothed jaguars, of vultures circling overhead, waiting to clean up after the kill. "Oh, for pity's sake, Daisy Bell," she muttered, shivering under the blazing sun. She was drenched in perspiration. "Act your age for once!"

But age had nothing to do with it. The noise behind her was not just her imagination. Something was definitely there, and it was gaining on her.

Farm animals, she assured herself again, not believing it any more this time than she did the last. A rational woman would wait and see what was there before hitting the panic button. A rational woman would have signed up for one of those jungle-walk things—at least then she would've known what was out there.

Out *here,* she corrected silently, panting as she bent over the handlebars and pedaled furiously. And a rational person wouldn't be cursed with a hyperactive imagination in the first place.

It was a deer. Or a cow. It was a goat that had chewed its way out of its pen. Come to think of it, she'd seen a whole flock of the things beside one of the houses on the way to Tulum.

"Goats," she muttered. "Good gosh, of course!" But she didn't slow up, not even when she struck a larger-than-usual pothole.

"*¡Señorita! ¡Espéreme!*"

That was no goat. "Oh, God..." One look over her shoulder was enough to send her heart slamming into her throat. The man looked utterly wild. Waving one hand, he was racing after her, yelling at the top of his lungs.

"*¡Ayuda! ¡Espéreme, señorita—ayuda!*"

She didn't see a gun, but that didn't mean he didn't have one. She wasn't about to take any chances. Just yesterday she'd overheard a couple of the realtors from

Ontario talking about the drug problem and wondering how many millions of dollars worth of drugs ran right up the coastal highway.

That highway was less than a quarter of a mile inland from this scrubby little back road. If she'd accidentally stumbled into something—

"Oh, God, please," she panted as she put on a fresh burst of speed.

"¡P'favor, señorita—mi esposa—mi bebé—está gravemente enferma!" There was more, all of it screamed in the most terrifying voice she'd ever heard as the man ran after her, barefoot, his long hair streaming out from under a filthy duck-billed cap. Surely the village couldn't be too many miles away—if she could only reach it first, someone would help her. He was crazy! Dangerous!

Pale despite her fading sunburn, she flung a look over her shoulder. He was falling behind, thank God, but still running, still screaming at her. Mouth dry with fear, she turned back just in time to see the rocks scattered across the path like a pile of gray watermelons that had fallen from a truck.

Desperately she twisted the wheel, but it was too late. Sailing cleanly over the handlebars, she landed hard on her knees, hands and right cheek, and skidded several feet before collapsing.

Pain ripped through her like flames as she struggled to suck air into her lungs. Had she broken anything? There was no time to find out—she had to get away!

He was on her before she could even catch her breath. Hurling himself on top of her, he began babbling even as he rolled her over. Not until he dragged her to her feet, though, did she see the knife.

It was enormous. He didn't even bother to take it out of his belt, knowing that the sight of it would send her into shock. With her lungs bursting for air, half-a-dozen abrasions burning like fire, and both her legs broken for all she knew, Daisy was no match for the powerful stocky young Mexican.

"Just stop yelling at me, dammit!" she cried when she could catch her breath.

But he didn't. Dragging her into the bushes, he kept going on and on about his damned *gravemente enfermos,* yelling into her ear while he pushed her along in front of him or pulled her behind him. The smell of sweat, beer and cheap cologne made her stomach revolt.

"Just shut up! You don't scare me one little bit, you sweating pig!"

She might as well have saved her breath. On and on it went—the man was obviously demented. *"¡Gravement enferma, si!"*

What the devil was a *gravemente enferma*? A government inferno? Grave—cemetary. Crematory? God, no! Think, Daisy, think! Grave, gravement—engraving?

Engraving. Counterfeiting! She'd been captured by a band of counterfeiters! But where did the inferno come in?

God help her, she was going to find out, because unless she could think of some way to get that knife away from him, she didn't stand a snowball's chance in hell.

Ten minutes later, Daisy had her wind back, if not her nerve. Her kidnapper seemed to have run down and hadn't spoken another word. After what felt like an interminable length of time, but was probably only a few minutes, they came to an almost invisible trail. After that, the going was slightly easier, although she was already scraped, scratched and punctured on every visible inch of her body. By tomorrow, half her wounds would probably be infected, the other half oozing and itching from some weird tropical version of poison ivy.

Calm down now—just think, Daisy—for once in your life, try to think your way through something before you barge in and make it worse!

All right, all right, she was thinking! He had the knife out—now and then he had to use it to whack through a vine or a branch that came down over the trail. If she could watch for a chance and move fast enough, she might be able to jerk her wrist free and make a break for it.

But how far could she get before he caught her? He knew these jungles better than she did, and if she thought he was bad now, what would he be like if she made him mad?

On the other hand, her legs were twice as long as his. She could run faster. How far could a person throw an enormous knife in thick jungle?

Too big a coward to risk finding out, Daisy told herself that she'd do better to wait until they reached their destination. They were obviously headed *somewhere.* If there was anyone there who spoke English— preferably someone sane—she might be able to bargain with them. She had her credit cards. They could have her entire bank balance—not a whole lot, but in pesos it would sound astronomical. The business had increased in value considerably since they first started it on her divorce settlement and money Cora Joan's aunt had left her. They could probably raise some more money on that, if they had to, but it would take time. What if her captors didn't want to wait?

No, dammit, she'd see them in hell first! Daisy Chains was all she had, and she was not going to lose it!

Blinded with sweat, she tripped over a root and then swore when a thorny vine grabbed the side of her shorts and ripped. She swore again. She prayed. She stubbornly refused to cry.

Why me, Lord? Is it because I skipped church twice in a row last month?

Yes, why her? Granted, she was paying a small fortune to lie around doing nothing while all around her, decent hardworking people slaved away under the most primitive conditions for a few pesos a day. Which automatically made her guilty, she supposed.

On the other hand, there were other resorts up and down the beach—some of them far more expensive. Why not pick on someone from Club Aventura? Or that hotel with the big fancy entrance?

"Look, I don't mean to question your judgment or anything like that," she gasped over her shoulder, "but why me? Some of the other folks staying at the hotel drive their own Jaguars, did you know that?"

And not one of them would be caught dead pedaling a pink-and-orange bicycle down a dinky little cow path, she reminded herself.

"I understand a few of them flew their own jets to Cancun—and did you know there's a man and his wife—" his mistress, more likely "—who're staying aboard their own yacht at the hotel pier?"

Not that she wished them any ill fortune, but dammit, why did it have to be her? She wasn't among the idle rich. She clipped grocery coupons like a frugal housewife and bought practically every stitch she wore at factory-outlet stores!

"Why me?"

"¡Dése prisa!"

"Okay, okay, because I was stupid enough to go traipsing off into the boondocks on my own, and any idiot knows that that's just asking for trouble. Sorry I asked."

She plodded on, swatting mosquitoes, wiping sweat from her eyes with a scratched arm—and swearing under her breath. Her kidnapper was younger than she'd thought at first. Younger and stronger. At first he had been alternately pushing her before him and dragging her along by both wrists, but the third time she tripped and nearly fell, he'd eased his grip. Now he was only crushing the bones in her left wrist.

At least she'd still be able to sign a check, she thought with a sudden urge to giggle. Just what she needed now—hysterics. Daisy felt a strange sense of unreality ease over her. So this was how it was all going to end. Would anyone ever know? Would anyone even wonder what had happened to her? They were so far off the beaten track she could scream her head off and not be heard. Her body might never be found.

An image of those great black vultures perched in a dead tree returned, and she shivered, despite the sweltering heat. She was too exhausted to go farther. "If you're going to kill me, just do it and get it over with! I'm not budging another inch!"

Leaning back against a tree, she closed her eyes and struggled to catch her breath, half expecting the ax—or rather, the knife—to fall. When it didn't, she opened one eye. And then the other.

He was waiting with ill-disguised impatience, nervously running his thumb over the sharp edge of his knife blade. Abruptly he jammed it back into the rope that held up his ragged trousers and cut loose with a spate of words, none of which she understood.

Then, grabbing her arm, he again urged her forward. *"¿Quiere que vayamos?"*

"Oh, for God's sake, don't you speak any English at all?"

But he was already off and running, dragging her after him. *"¡Dése prisa, señorita, dése prisa!"*

And day-say pree-sah to you, too, you bloodthirsty creep, Daisy fumed hopelessly as she stumbled along in his wake. It was either that or have her arm wrenched from its socket.

But then, why should she have expected him to speak her language when she didn't speak his? Irritated that her innate sense of fairness would kick in at a time like this, she jerked her arm away, but didn't try to escape. For the hundredth time since the nightmare had begun, she asked herself, *Why me?*

It was that blasted attitude she'd worked so hard to perfect. It had to be! The haircut, the gaudy jewelry— that drop-dead look she had practiced for so long in front of her bathroom mirror before she'd ever worked up enough nerve to try it out....

Beau used to tell her she had about as much class as a wet-nosed mongrel. Toward the end, when he'd been trying to force her to divorce him so that he wouldn't have to give her a penny—despite the fact that she'd worked all those years while he had been going to school—he'd ridiculed the way she walked, the way she talked, and most of all, the way she dressed. He'd told her he never should have married a woman so much older than he was, that she was an embarrassment to him.

She'd been determined to show him. Long after he had ceased to matter to her, she'd still been trying. As if by dressing the part and pretending to be someone she wasn't, she could heal the old wounds.

Well, the wounds had healed of their own accord, and somewhere along the way, Daisy had discovered that it was really quite easy to keep people at a distance. And by keeping them at a distance, she didn't have to deal with them.

Dealing with people had never been particularly easy for her. Once her marriage had started coming apart, it had become even worse. Until she'd discovered the attitude. Granted, it was a little lonely, but it was a heck of a lot safer in the long run. And Daisy had had it with the short run.

"¡Dése prisa, señorita! Mi esposa gravemente enferma."

But Daisy was no longer listening. Before they even entered the clearing, she could hear the screams. A woman's screams.

"Oh, God, please, no," she whimpered. Not torture! She hated pain! She'd end up crying and begging, stripped of what little pride she had left! *Oh, Gardiner, I never got to tell you how wonderful you really are—I never even got to know you, and now it's too late!*

Fresh sweat broke out on her face, stinging the raw place where she had slid along the rocky path on her cheekbone. When her knees threatened to give way on her, her captor loosened his iron grip on her wrist and grabbed one hand instead, dragging her through the last few yards of dense undergrowth.

"How's your friend's sunburn today?"

It took Gardiner a moment to realize that the blonde from Dallas was speaking to him, and not to one of the other people who were also waiting for tables in the dining room.

"I beg your pardon?" It must be catching, he thought with a wry smile. Just thinking about her was enough to make him start talking the way she did. Hoity-toity. "Uh . . . my friend?"

"The good-looking one. What is she, a model or something? Should I know her? I saw you two together at breakfast the other day, and I said to Harvey, that girl's got to be a model. Even when she's wearing blue jeans, she's got that certain look about her. Oh, my gosh, I sure hope she didn't go and ruin her complexion, getting blistered that way. I told her Harvey always made me soak in strong tea—his mama did it to him, and he's a redhead, you know how they always burn—but she said you had this other stuff, so—"

"Uh, yes, she's better now. By the way, you haven't seen her lately, have you? We seem to have got our signals crossed on where we were to meet."

"Not since this morning. I saw her talking to the assistant rec director over there by the front desk. Isn't she in her room?"

But Gardiner didn't wait around to answer. He'd been stopping by her room all afternoon, first knocking on the front door, then the back, calling through her louvered windows. He'd checked in the office, and her name wasn't on any of the lists for scheduled tours. She wasn't on the beach, and the guy at the concession stand claimed she hadn't been there all day, or he'd have noticed.

The bike stand. That must be it.

"Hey, aren't you going to wait for a table?" the pink-faced blonde called after him.

"I'll be back later. Just thought of something I need to do."

Pedaling fast and inexpertly, Gardiner told himself he was crazy. Crazy to be worried about some woman he hardly knew just because she'd been gone for six hours. Crazy to think he was responsible for her welfare when she'd let him know in pretty clear terms that she could look after herself, thanks.

Crazy to be thinking about her, period. The damned woman was becoming an obsession, and the last thing he needed at this point in his life was another female obsession!

It was still light, but the sun was already brushing the treetops. Once it dropped out of sight, dark would come almost instantly. Especially here in the boonies, surrounded by banana groves and swamps and vines big enough to trip an elephant.

The highway was less than half a mile to his left. He could hear the occasional sound of a passing vehicle. To his right, he caught the glint of light on the water and the infrequent flash of a sail on the horizon. Sunset in the tropics. So peaceful-looking.

But Gardiner knew that looks could be deceptive. He'd seen other palm trees silhouetted against another sunset, some twenty-odd years ago and half a world away.

At least there were no land mines here. No snipers. No Charlie patrol to rise up out of a rice paddy like small tattered ghosts. Even so, it was rough enough. Barely passable in some places, with boulders and blowholes and pits filled with broken coral that could roll under your feet and throw you if you didn't watch your step.

God, what if she'd wandered down to the beach and fallen? She could have twisted her ankle—she might be lying there in excruciating pain even now, unable to call out, unable to get help....

He tried calling her name several times. Silence echoed back. Even the surf was quiet as the last warm breeze whispered away.

There was a growing hollowness in his gut of the sort he hadn't felt in a long, long time. He didn't want to remember Nam—he'd dealt with that and closed the book on it. Instead, he thought about all the times he used to go spelunking with a gang of older kids when he visited his grandparents in the eastern part of West Virginia. He couldn't have been more than twelve. His mother had died when he was seven, and he'd run pretty wild after that, except for the times he visited his grandparents.

Even then, he'd managed to slip away. He wasn't used to living under a woman's thumb. Growing up in an all-male household, he'd gotten used to ''going with the guys.'' And the guys had thought exploring the many limestone caves in the area was the test of a real man. As the son of a coal miner, it should have come naturally to all the Gentry boys. But to Gardiner, it never had.

Not that he'd been scared, exactly. He'd simply hated it. He had gone along only to prove he was as good as the next guy, but he'd hated the smell of mud, the feel of slime, the darkness, the constant uncertainty. Hated knowing he was crawling along under tons of earth, with no easy way out if he panicked.

He'd never panicked—not quite. But at the age of fifteen, he'd sworn that one of these days he was going to get the hell out of Welch, West Virginia, and find some way to make a living that was clean, dry and above ground.

And he had. Thanks to a football scholarship, a stint in the army, and a few thousand hours of slogging over the books, working odd jobs and living on four hours of sleep a night.

He'd never once regretted it, but it hadn't come easy—Gardiner was no natural scholar. At a time when his younger brothers had been raising hell or starting families, he'd had too little time for pleasure, or for women—too little time for anything but work.

God, what was he doing here? He had no business taking a vacation—

In the gathering dusk, he almost ran over the bike before he saw it. The pink-and-orange coloring identified it only as hotel property, but there was no mistaking that chunk of silver-and-turquoise lying between two of the smaller rocks. The last time he'd seen it, it had been dangling just below a certain battered Panama hat.

Gardiner was off his own bike and on his knees before the wheels had stopped turning, looking for some sign of where she had gone. She had obviously been thrown when she'd struck those rocks, but how hard? Hard enough to knock her senseless? Hard enough to disorient her?

There was a streak of blood on one of the large flat-topped rocks. It could be from a scraped knee—or it could be from something far more serious.

He called her name. He got down on his hands and knees and tried to determine from the one small smear of dried blood the extent of her injuries and how long ago they had occurred, but he wasn't a cop. Just a lousy, impractical, useless math teacher!

At least she was ambulatory—that was something. Because she sure as hell hadn't waited around to be found, nor had he passed her on the road to the hotel.

"Oh, yeah—that's sure something, all right," he muttered. At this very minute, with night coming down hard, she could be wandering around this green, snake-infested sauna without a clue as to where she was or where to go to find help! She could have broken something, dammit—she could be crawling on all fours, trying to reach the village, bleeding . . .

Sweet Jesus, she could be dead.

"Daisy! Dammit, Daisy Valentine, where are you? Move something! *Do* something so I can find you!"

Cold with sweat, he began searching the edges of the road for a track, a sign. Anything that would give him a clue as to which way she'd gone. When he saw the print of a large bare foot in the powdery dust between a patch of grass and the pile of rocks, he felt a hand close over his heart and squeeze painfully.

And then, suddenly, he was back in another jungle, unarmed and with night coming on, desperately trying to locate some clue that would lead him back to his own unit without dropping him into one of the deadly bamboo-spiked pitfalls along the way. Crouching, he began to search the edge of the path for a broken twig, a bent stalk . . . a drop of blood.

Seven

—

It had been an unbelievable few hours. Daisy flexed her weary shoulders, tilted her head back for a moment and closed her eyes. Then, kneeling, she placed the fat wriggling infant in his mother's arms. Both she and the woman were laughing—or crying. She wasn't sure which, even now. All she knew was that Josephina's enormous black eyes were brimming as she cradled her newborn son and her smile was so beautiful it hurt.

Daisy mopped her own wet cheeks. "Talk about the blind leading the blind," she murmured as she began cleaning up after the hours-long ordeal that, incredibly, had produced a perfect baby boy with ten perfect fingers and ten perfect toes and one prefect little...

Well, whatever. Tomas had examined his new son from stem to stern, fallen to his knees beside his little

Josephina and wept openly. Then he had stumbled outside, where he'd finished the job he'd begun earlier in the day—that of drinking himself insensible.

Not that she blamed him. Daisy could have done with a stiff drink or two herself. Even coffee would have helped. "What will you call him?" she asked the exhausted woman-child who was now resting comfortably in the hammock, her baby lying across her breast. "That is, um—*que nombre?*"

Somehow, in the heat of the moment, she had managed to learn enough Spanish to get by. She knew, for instance, that the woman's *nombre* was Josephina, and that her husband's *nombre* was Tomas. Somehow, they had managed to communicate with a mixture of words and gestures. Some things transcended the need for words.

Josephina couldn't have been much more than sixteen, if Daisy was any judge—although Tomas looked to be well into his twenties. Still, it was Josephina who had hung in there, breathing and not bearing down, or bearing down and not breathing. Daisy, nearly hyperventilating as she'd tried to demonstrate, had done her best to remember all the bits and pieces she'd picked up from various television shows.

Then, too, she'd had a blow-by-blow description from more than a few of her married friends. Their whole social set had been busy reproducing back during the time when she and Beau had been waiting for him to graduate, and then to get established. Daisy had gone to baby shower after baby shower and then gone home to cry herself to sleep.

Glancing out the open doorway, she saw Tomas sprawled in drunken splendor near the chicken pen, the empty bottle lying beside him. Poor Tomas. She had misjudged him badly—the man had simply been terrified. From all she could make out, Josephina had been in labor with their first child half the night and all day, and according to Tomas, it wasn't supposed to be that way—his own mother popped them out like shelling peas.

Of course, she also learned that Tomas was the middle child of eleven. There was something to be said for experience, after all.

Daisy suspected that he'd be in no shape to lead her back to the road, even if she could have woken him up. Not that she was too eager to venture back into that sweltering jungle again—especially in the pitch dark. Tomorrow would do as well. No one would miss her—except perhaps the bicycle vendor.

Tiredly, she went about cleaning up, sending the occasional gloating look at the pair on the hammock. Tomas's hammock was still looped against the wall. He'd hardly be needing it tonight, but after only a moment's consideration, Daisy made up her mind to borrow Josephina's spare blanket and spread it out on the floor, instead. Her back was still a little too tender to sleep on it comfortably—especially in a woven hemp hammock.

Although, at the moment, anything even faintly horizontal looked inviting. She could have easily curled up on the bare ground between Tomas and the chicken pen and been asleep before her head even touched the ground.

It was hot and still. At first she thought it was the droning mosquito that had roused her from a sound

sleep. She sat up, and after a few groggy moments realized that it had been Tomas, who had awakened and
come inside, tripping over her legs in the process.

And dammit, he'd wakened Josephina and the baby!

"Shh," she cautioned as he stumbled to his knees
beside his wife and son.

"Lo siento, señorita," the man apologized. By the
light of the single candle, she watched him reverently
lift his son and cradle him in his arms. He sighed nois-
ily.

Daisy yawned. "Is he wet? Uh . . . *agua?* No, no—
pantalón?"

"No, no, señorita."

The baby made a whimpering sound. Josephina
snored softly. Tomas began to squirm, the baby still
held in his arms as he rose awkwardly to his feet.

"Do you want me to get him back to sleep?" asked
Daisy. She was too tired for this, really. From the way
he was lurching around, poor Tomas was still three
sheets to the wind—but if he dropped that baby, she
would personally see to it that he could never father
another one.

Tensely, she watched, ready to reach out and catch
little Tomas, Junior, as his father unhooked his own
hammock and stretched it across the tiny room. Within
minutes, he too, was snoring, with the baby lying
across his chest.

Josephina muttered something in her sleep, and
Junior began to whimper louder. Tomas patted him on
the rump with a dark callused hand that, to Daisy's
knowledge, had not been washed all day.

She stared at the small family group, feeling something uncomfortably close to envy. Drying vegetables

and assorted clothing hung from the thatched roof. A lizard skittered across the wall, which was made of peeled saplings. It was a far cry from the gleaming, toy-stuffed nurseries of her friends. In fact, the sleeping arrangements alone would probably horrify any expert on pediatric and maternal care, but then, they didn't know everything.

And, anyway, who was she to interfere? With Tomas's machete propped up in the corner, she wasn't about to wrestle him for possession of his son.

Gathering up her blanket, she moved outside. There had been a tiny current of air funneling through the doors of the hut. Outside, the air was perfectly still. Mosquitoes droned. She could roll up in her blanket and suffocate, or she could let them chew on her.

While she tried to make up her mind, a tree frog croaked—and then another. At least the pigs were penned up for the night, and the chickens had gone to roost at dark. If anything else should come crashing through the jungle, she would just have to take her chances. She was too tired to run.

She was too tired to get back to sleep, too. But even worse than that, she was sticky. She felt as if she hadn't had a bath in three weeks.

A quarter moon had risen less than an hour ago. In its feeble light, she could barely make out the water barrel. Not stopping to think twice, she sat up and began peeling out of her clothes. Dammit, she deserved something for all she'd been through! She didn't intend to drink the stuff, but if it was good enough for the pigs and chickens to drink, it was good enough for her to bathe in.

A towel she could do without, but she'd have killed for a bar of soap. Or even a set of fresh underwear. Still, five gourds full of tepid water poured slowly over her head and body went a long way toward restoring her spirits.

Next, she rinsed out her panties and bra and slung them over Josephina's clothesline. By that time, she had dried off and reluctantly put on her shorts and shirt again. Naked had felt wonderful. Oh, how she wished she were the type to sleep that way, but she wasn't. Never had been. Some inhibitions were harder to shed than others.

Within minutes after she buttoned her orange shorts and Hawaiian-print camp shirt and spread her blanket out again on the smoothest stretch of hard pebbly ground she could find, she was asleep.

Once more something had aroused her. The baby? Tomas's snores? Or had Josephina called out? "Josephina? I'm out here—did you need me? Uh—*necedida?*" No, that wasn't right, but it was close enough.

It came again—little Tomas. He whimpered and then howled, and Daisy, who had wanted to get her hands on the precious little bundle again ever since she'd handed him over to his mother, needed no further invitation. Josephina needed her rest, she rationalized as she tiptoed inside. Tomas must have thought so, too, but in his state, he could easily roll over and dump the poor darling onto the floor. If that baby got hurt, he'd never forgive himself. Nor would Josephina.

It would be much better if she... "Go back to sleep, Tomas, I'll look after him for a little while," she whispered as she lifted the tiny bundle away from his father's lax arms. It was too hot to sleep so close, anyway. The precious little dumpling was wringing wet with perspiration.

Perspiration? Maybe not.

Thank goodness there were plenty of diapers. The old-fashioned cloth kind. Feeling about in the dark, Daisy found the basket Josephina had shown her and lifted off the top, taking it outside with her. "There, there, darling love, Aunt Daisy's got you now, don't fuss so, hmm?"

He was adorable! Brown as a chinquapin, plump as a pigeon, and so beautiful she could look at him and weep. Those two children in there—for they were little more than that, really—might live in a house made of sticks and grass, with only the most meager furnishings, they might seem to live a hand-to-mouth existence, growing a few vegetables, raising a few pigs and chickens, but they had something money couldn't buy. She had seen the stark terror in Tomas's eyes when he'd thought his Josephina had been deathly ill. *Gravemente enfermo.* She had seen the look of loving pride on little Josephina's face when she'd presented him with his son.

"Oh, damn," Daisy whispered, sniffling as she sat cross-legged on a blanket in the moonlight and rocked little Tomas, Junior, in her arms.

That was the sight that greeted Gardiner when he finally broke through into the clearing. It had taken him hours—thank God he'd had the foresight to bring along a flashlight! Growing up in an area riddled with caves and abandoned mines, it came as second nature when a man was searching for someone lost.

She threw up an arm to shield her eyes, and he switched it off and waited for his own eyes to recover. "Daisy?" he called softly, more to reassure her than to assure himself of her identity.

It came to him in the next few moments that his heart was pounding like hail on a tin roof. His legs felt like two strands of cooked spaghetti, and he was cursing under his breath. As soon as his night vision returned, he made his way across the clearing. It was a little late for caution now, after barging into the place with all the finesse of a wild boar.

"Hey, are you all right?" he asked softly.

"Shh, he's sleeping. I'm fine."

Who was sleeping? Her guard? Her kidnapper? Was she staked out as bait? Was he going to step on a mine or end up shish kebabbed on a punji stake before he reached her?

"Gardiner Gentry, I'd like you to meet my proudest accomplishment to date—his name will probably end up being something like Tomas, Junior, or whatever the Mexican equivalent is."

Whoa! A baby? Her proudest accomplishment? "You want to bring me into the picture here?" he murmured softly as he knelt at her side. It was a baby, all right. Black hair, like hers; brown eyes, like hers; dark skin, not like hers. Besides, if she'd been all that pregnant, then he'd better go back and repeat basic biology from page one.

"Day-zee, *mi bebe, por favor?*"

"*Una momento, Josephina.*"

Gardiner's eyebrows—both of them—peaked like a pair of pup tents. A few hours away from the hotel, and suddenly, she was producing babies and rattling off Spanish like a native?

When she rose gracefully from the blanket, still holding the infant, and disappeared inside, Gardiner started to follow. Somebody damned well owed him a few answers around here! He hadn't wasted an entire afternoon worrying over her and then added ten years to his age following her trail through this pygmy jungle just to have her disappear on him!

"What on earth are you doing here?" she asked softly as she turned and barged into him, backing him out through the doorway.

"What the hell do you think I'm doing here?" he growled.

"There aren't any ruins around here that I know of. Did you get lost?"

"There's a ruin, all right. You're looking at it."

It took her a minute, but when she realized that he'd come after her, Daisy uttered a low cry and leaned forward, resting the top of her head against his chest. They were both sitting cross-legged on her blanket now. "Oh, Gardiner—oh, Lord, I'm sorry. It didn't occur to me that anyone might worry. Not that I could have done anything about it, anyway—I mean, by the time Tomas and I got here, poor little Josephina was almost ready to go, and from then on I had my hands too full to think about anything else."

"You want to start at the beginning? We've got plenty of time. It shouldn't take more than a couple of hours to get back to the hotel—we'll make it easily before breakfast." His words were clipped. There was a steeliness about him that came though clearly, even in the darkness.

"You're angry with me, aren't you?" For some crazy reason, that made her feel like crying.

Instead, she pulled away and sat up straight, struggling to pull together the shreds of her old protective attitude. Sure, she was tired. Sure, she looked like hell. She'd been through the wringer and back again over the past few hours, but he didn't have to know. It was too dark to see, thank goodness.

"I suppose the bike boy was worried—he probably thought I'd stolen his precious bicycle and split for parts unknown. What do you suppose the penalty is for losing a rusty three-speed bike around here? Life imprisonment? A steady diet of jalapeños and—"

"What the devil were you thinking of, running off that way?"

"Look, I'm sorry if you've wasted your valuable time tracking me down, but it's hardly my fault. Nobody asked you to. Besides, how was I to know I'd hit a rock and get jumped by a madman with a machete and..."

She sighed. It sounded so farfetched, she couldn't blame him for the way he was staring at her. She wouldn't have believed it, either. But here she was. And there was little Tomas, Junior. And inside the hut, propped up in the corner, was that wicked knife that had scared her half to death. "Gardiner, I'm sorry if you went to any trouble on my account, but I didn't ask anyone to come looking for me. I would have been all right. Tomas would have taken me back to the road tomorrow."

"Trouble!" he fairly shouted.

"Hush! Do you want to wake the baby again? Dammit, it's not my fault you're angry—don't take your rotten temper out on me!'' She felt dangerously close to tears, and that would be the last straw.

"I'm not—" he began loudly, and then, when she slapped her hand over his mouth, he grabbed her wrist and shoved his face up to hers. In a harsh whisper, he said, "I am not angry with you, dammit. I was *worried!* No—that's a lie. I'm mad as hell, and I wasn't just worried, I was scared stiff! Would you mind telling me what the bloody hell happened? *What* madman? *What* machete? Are you being held prisoner? What's going on, for God's sake?''

And so she told him. Leaving out the terror she'd felt—the stunned disbelief that such a thing could be happening in broad daylight in a civilized country, a few miles away from several resort hotels. Leaving out her bruises and scrapes, which had been nothing compared with the sheer panic she'd felt at not even being able to communicate with her captor.

Calmly, she explained that Tomas was young, and this was his first baby, and he'd been so frantic about his wife that he'd gone running for help and flagged down the first person he'd seen—which had been her.

Of course, "flagging down" was hardly the appropriate description, but she didn't feel like going into details right now. She was still exhausted, and Gardiner was so close... Suddenly, she felt an overpowering need to curl up in his strong arms and let him worry about how to get them both back to civilization.

"So, I delivered it," she finished simply. "Not that he wouldn't have been born without me, but I was there. Mine were the first hands to hold him—and he's perfect, Gardiner, absolutely gorgeous. And so strong! He's got a grip like his daddy, bless his little heart.''

"What do you know about his daddy's grip?"

"Oh, well, I . . ." And then she yawned. Her shoulders slumped. "What time is it, anyway? I feel like I've been here forever."

It was only a bit past midnight. She'd been there for less than eight hours—eight of the most terrifying, most exhilarating, most gratifying hours of her life. "Would you mind very much if I took a nap before we started back? You wouldn't believe how exhausting childbirth can be."

It was Gardiner who moved the blanket to a pile of dried grass, gathered and waiting to be used on another roof. It was Gardiner who tucked up a smaller bundle of the grass and poked it under her head for a pillow.

And it was Gardiner who came down beside her, turned his back and went to sleep while she was still lying there marveling over the fact that she, Daisy Valentine, ex-dowdy housewife, was sleeping in a jungle under a tropical moon, alongside a man who looked like a cross between Richard Gere and Ted Danson— and that she'd just delivered a baby alone and unaided.

Let's see you top that one, Meryl Streep.

The mosquito battalion returned just before dawn. The air had turned surprisingly cool. Shivering, Daisy swatted impotently without opening her eyes, not wanting to become fully conscious of her growing discomfort. She'd never been a particularly happy camper.

"'Smatter, honey?" Gardiner murmured sleepily. He hadn't moved an inch all night. Dammit, why should he? He was all snug and barricaded in his khaki slacks, his white wool socks, and a shirt that covered his arms. All she had was her shorts, her camp shirt and her sandals.

"Nothing," she grumbled. "Absolutely nothing. Shut up and go back to sleep."

Something in her tone of voice must have alerted him to the fact that she wasn't telling the absolute truth. The dried grass beneath them crackled and she felt a growing warmth along her backside as he rolled over onto his side. "Move out to the edge as far as you can," he whispered.

"The edge of what? The earth?"

"The blanket. That is, unless you want to go on offering yourself up as a human sacrifice to those bloodthirsty little devils all night."

She moved. He moved right behind her, cradling her on the curve of his body, and then he flipped the rest of the blanket over the top of them.

Within seconds, Daisy forgot all about cold morning air and trophy-size mosquitoes, and started thinking of all the reasons that lying snuggled up against the hard body of a handsome virile man—a man she was already dangerously attracted to—was not particularly smart.

Fortunately, she was still too drowsy to do anything about it.

"Daisy?"

"Mmm?"

"You asleep?"

She wasn't—far from it. But she thought it better to pretend.

"I missed you." And when she didn't say anything, he went on, "These past few days haven't been as much fun." The arm that had been resting over her waist curled around her body, drawing her even closer. It was something new—the closeness. Beau had not been a demonstrative man. Five minutes for sex twice a week and he was snoring. And then once a week. And then once a month. After the first two years of their marriage, sex had consisted of an occasional pat on the rear end when he was in an expansive mood—and then even that ended.

Daisy moved one of her feet and encountered one of Gardiner's. He was still wearing his deck shoes. Quickly, he shucked them off and captured her foot between his, and Daisy felt a flutter in her belly that was neither gas nor heartburn. Hunger, maybe—it occurred to her that she hadn't eaten in nearly twenty-four hours.

But it wasn't hunger for food that had her staring out into the darkness, shockingly aware of every square inch of contact between their two bodies.

"Blanket's too short. It won't cover both ends," Gardiner whispered.

"We could, um, bury our feet under the grass, I suppose." The hand on the end of the arm was now splayed across her stomach, burning through the single thin layer of cotton. Daisy wondered if a print of his palm would permanently mark the place.

"Wouldn't recommend it. Too much livestock in there."

She stiffened. "Livestock?"

"Shh, don't wake the baby."

In a tangle of knees and elbows, she managed to turn over. "What do you mean, livestock?" she whispered back.

"Nothing you need to worry about."

"Then why did you—"

"Daisy, hush up, huh?"

"But what did you mean? Bugs? Snakes? What, Gardiner?"

With a groan, he straightened and pulled her tightly against him, shutting off her questions in the most practical way. Before the kiss had even got off the ground, Daisy knew she was in over her head. She'd been married for four years, she'd dated occasionally both before her marriage and after her divorce, and she saw every romantic movie that came to town—not even her best friend knew that about her.

But none of that had prepared her for the sheer masculine intensity of Gardiner Gentry. He was like an electromagnetic force field. She barely knew the man, yet she couldn't have resisted him if her life had depended on it.

Beginning with deceptive gentleness, he parted her lips, tasting, caressing, coercing, seducing. Slowly, with the daring finesse of a practiced raider, he ravished her mouth. There was no other word to describe it.

Daisy, struggling with her own desires and inadequacies, real and imagined, had no way of knowing that his very intensity was the culmination of years of the kind of loneliness that only a man like Gardiner could know—and days of watching Daisy Valentine pretending to be something she wasn't.

And God help him he wanted them both—the shy, funny, spunky woman who was hiding under all that paint and funky hardware, and the tall striking beauty who could cut her hair with a Weed Eater and still look like a million dollars. He wanted it all!

Her breasts were crushed against his chest, and he was hard—everywhere. His hands moved slowly over her back, his fingers combing through the fringe of dark silk that curled in her nape, and then moving down to curve over her bottom, cupping her, drawing her closer to the heat of his throbbing groin.

Daisy was trembling, but not from the cold. Somehow, she managed to get one arm around his neck, but it wasn't enough—she wanted to be closer. She wanted to absorb him. She wanted to be inside him.

She wanted him inside her.

No words were spoken—none were needed. Gardiner knew what she wanted because he wanted it, too. More than he'd ever wanted anything in his life, he wanted this tall, exquisite, exasperating woman. It scared the hell out of him to want anything so much.

Unable to help himself, he moved over her, parting her thighs with his knee. They were both fully dressed. He stared down at her, seeing her exotic features come slowly into focus in the gray predawn light. Her eyes were clinging to his, as if she were pleading with him.

"I know, I know—sweetheart, I know," he ground out between clenched teeth.

Daisy stared up at his tightly drawn face. It was just beginning to grow light. She could see the sharp edge of his cheekbones, sharper now than ever. The lips that had just stolen her soul right out of her body looked strangely grim, almost as if he were angry.

She felt his fingers fumbling at the buttons of her shirt, and when he cursed under his breath, she slid her

hands under his and finished the job herself. She was
aching to feel his touch on her naked flesh. To feel his
lips on her. To feel—

"Daisy, sweetheart, this isn't going to work."

"Yes, it is—I'll help you. It'll work just fine."

"Honey—"

"If you just shift over a little bit, I can . . ." Hearing
her own words, she cringed. Good old Daisy—wanting to give more of herself than anyone wanted to take.
Oh, God, would she never learn?

Gardiner felt her withdraw even before she pushed
him none too gently off to one side. He eased as far
away as the small space permitted, his flesh aching and
angry at being denied. How the devil did a man handle a situation like this? It had never come up before—Lord knew he wasn't the most experienced of
men, but he'd thought he had better sense than to start
something he couldn't finish and leave them both
hanging this way.

"Daisy, honey, it's—"

"It's nothing. For goodness' sake, Gardiner, don't
look so grim. Did you think I've never been kissed before?"

Attempting clumsily to adjust his clothes without
being too obvious about it, he considered changing his
mind. But it was no good. The mood was shattered,
and if he was honest, he'd have to admit that he had
done it deliberately.

In the first place, he didn't have protection for her—
it had been twenty years since he'd been in the habit of
carrying something in his wallet. In the second place,
somebody inside the house was beginning to stir
around. And desperate or not, he couldn't picture

either one of them being comfortable with the idea of making love before an audience.

But it was the third place that settled matters for him. He'd learned the hard way that sex didn't always equate to love. Before he put himself on the firing line again, he was going to be damned sure he knew what he was getting involved in.

Being dumped by Georgia Riggs had hurt, sure, but he knew now that it had only been a surface wound. He'd been embarrassed, not to mention mad as hell at having made such a fool of himself over some hot-looking kid with an appetite for older men.

Getting dumped by a woman like Daisy Valentine was another matter. A wound like that wouldn't heal overnight. In fact, it might not heal at all.

Daisy crawled out from under the blanket and brushed herself off, not meeting his eyes. ''Do you suppose we could ask for a few tortillas before we get out of here? I hate to be indelicate, but my stomach's growling like a circus lion. All I can think of is food.''

''Yeah, sure. Me, too.''

He was hungry, all right, only not for breakfast. But food would have to suffice, because he wasn't about to give in to the real hunger that was gnawing at him—not without giving it a whole lot of thought first.

Eight

————

Beans, hoecakes and coffee. It may have been Mexican, but it was Southern country, too. Back home, Daisy would have eaten her corn bread with buttermilk instead of honey, and her pintos would have been topped with chopped onion instead of chili peppers, but the coffee was very much like that her grandfather used to make—strong enough to climb a tree and let out a rebel yell.

"Is he sleeping?" she asked Josephina. She'd been horrified to discover her patient up and playing hostess at the crack of dawn, but no amount of arguing, even with Gardiner to translate, had changed the new mother's mind.

"Si. ¿El es magnífico, no?"

Daisy smiled right down to her toenails. *"El es magnífico, si,"* she replied, and took a swallow of the goat's milk Gardiner had poured for her earlier.

"Don't melt your fillings," he murmured, too low for the new parents to hear, especially as they were once more hanging over their son's improvised cradle.

She deliberately shoveled up a forkload of beans, making sure there were several peppers on top. After last night she had some fences to mend, and the sooner she started the better. "What are you looking at?" she muttered when she could breathe again.

"Is the smoke that's coming out of your ears caused by your temper, or is it just the peppers?"

"Is playing Boy Scout what makes you sound like a twelve-year-old, or are you always this way?"

He grinned and continued to eat. Daisy ate and continued to burn. As for Josephina and Tomas, they continued to hang over their son's tiny bed and gloat, and watching them, Daisy felt tears fill her eyes.

The peppers, of course. What else could it be?

By eight o'clock, the sun had burned the dewy freshness off the day. Looking around her at the neatly scraped yard around the one-room thatched-roof house, the flock of chickens busily scratching at the edge of the clearing, the rocky field of corn behind the house and the square patch of banana trees off to one side, Daisy felt a sense of unreality creep over her. Yesterday's events seemed more than ever like an Indiana Jones film. Things like that didn't happen in real life—not to Daisy Valentine, ex-housewife, struggling small-town entrepreneur. It was all a wide-screen stereophonic dream brought on by too much highly seasoned food.

As for what had happened during the night, she knew damned good and well she'd dreamed that, because if she'd thought for one minute that she had helped a man undress her and then begged him to take her, she would dig a hole, crawl into it and die!

But of course, she had. Which was why Gardiner was watching her now as if she were some strange new life-form he couldn't quite pin a label on. And why she was feeling so awfully vulnerable.

"More coffee, Daisy?" he asked.

"I don't believe so, thank you," she replied, delicately blotting her lips on her shirttail.

"Why don't you say your goodbyes to *mamacita* and son while I have a few words with Tomas? We ought to be getting back before they send out the Mounties."

Goodbye? Just like that? Daisy felt her sinuses begin to clog up again as she rose and went around to where Josephina knelt over the baby. "Could I hold him one last time, Josephina? *Por favor?*"

Maybe it was the outstretched arms—or maybe it was the expression on her face. The Mexican woman needed no explanations. Smiling, she lifted her son and placed him in Daisy's arms, and Daisy bent over him, crooning, admiring, marveling that something that, only a few hours ago had been so red and wet and funny-looking, could be transformed so swiftly into something so rare and beautiful.

Outside, Gardiner talked to Tomas. Tomas talked to Gardiner. Josephina leaned in the doorway and listened openly, not interrupting, and Daisy tucked a small sliver of her heart into the tiny brown fingers, kissing each one in turn as she said goodbye to her baby.

Both Gardiner and Daisy were quiet on the trek back through the jungle to the road. It was just as well—

Daisy was feeling dangerously emotional. She was in no condition to deal sensibly with any possible attraction she might feel toward Gardiner Gentry.

They went single file on the narrow, all-but-invisible trail. When, now and then, Gardiner would stop and hold a branch for her to pass, she avoided looking at his face. Instead, she looked at his hands, and then wished she hadn't.

Just because a man had nice hands didn't prove anything.

Dammit, Beau had had nice hands. At least, they'd been clean and well kept—professionally manicured, in fact. Smoother even than her own. And he'd turned out to be a weak, ambitious, philandering jerk whose greatest skill was zinging her with subtle emotional barbs. Half the time, she hadn't even known she'd been wounded until she was practically bleeding to death.

So much for nice hands.

"Tomas said to tell you he was sorry if he frightened you."

"Wha—? Oh. *Now* he tells me."

"Were you frightened?"

"Me? Why should I have been frightened? Just because some yelling waving maniac comes crashing out of the bushes and drags me off into the jungle?" She was trying desperately to be cool, but it wasn't coming off. For one thing, she wasn't dressed for it. The chic sports ensemble she'd put on fresh the morning before showed a remarkable record of everything she'd been through since then.

And then there was the way Gardiner kept looking at her. It wasn't exactly a smile, but there was something in his eyes...

Suffice to say, they no longer reminded her of stainless steel. "I was petrified," she confessed. "At first I thought I'd stumbled into some sort of a drug deal or something. If I could have talked to him—or better yet, understood what he was saying—it might have been different, but all I could see was this half-mad terrorist armed with a wicked-looking machete, who seemed to think I was his personal retirement plan. He kept shouting something about inferno engravings, and I thought he was going on about the stupid gringa woman who was going to make him richer than his wildest dreams."

Gardiner chuckled. "You did," he said, holding aside a drooping vine.

Daisy brushed past him, feeling the brief contact all the way to the soles of her feet. "Did what? Make him rich?" A smile started slowly and then spread like the sunrise. "Yeah, I guess I did, didn't I? Gardiner, it was unbelievable! They're so sweet—all three of them. Even the pigs and chickens. And to think I almost missed them. What if I'd gone in the other direction? What if I had decided to sack out on the beach under a *palapa* instead of setting out for the village to paint?"

"No question about it, the course of human history would have been forever altered."

"Don't laugh at me, darn you. Gardiner, is there some way I could help them? I mean, do something sort of on a regular basis? Do you suppose I could set up some kind of a scholarship fund for little Tomas?"

They had just broken through onto the road, having collected Daisy's tote bag where she'd dropped it along the way. The bikes were nowhere in sight. Evidently one of the hotel employees who used the road to go back and forth to the village had recognized them and returned them both, thinking they had been abandoned.

"A scholarship fund, hmm? Aren't you getting just a little bit ambitious there?"

She turned in the direction of the hotel and continued to walk. With her bruised cheekbone, both knees scraped and sore and her body one big ache from sleeping on the ground, it was hardly the same saunter she had practiced in front of her mirror, but it served the purpose, which was to get her to the nearest bathtub and bed—preferably her own—as quickly as possible.

"Ambitious? I don't think so. I mean, I'm no rich gringa, though the shop is doing okay—oh, the cash flow wouldn't ransom a blowfly at this point, but we're slowly getting there, and we aren't exactly starving along the way. The point is, I don't have any dependents. No family at all. And little Tomas is only a day old, so by the time he's ready to go to school—"

"Little Joaquin Tomas Daisy Hayntree Mendoza is going to—"

"Dai-zee Hayn-tree! Are you serious?" She came to a dead halt and turned to gawk at him.

His eyes were sparkling, but there wasn't a glimmer of a smile on his face. "As I was saying, little J.T. is going to need a few things before then—things I've taken the liberty of arranging with—"

"What do you mean, *you've* taken the liberty of arranging? Tomas is *my* baby, not yours! You had absolutely no right to—"

"Call it a baby present. It's customary, isn't it?"

Tilting her head, Daisy eyed him skeptically. "Gardiner, were you serious about the names? Are they really going to name him for me?"

He grinned at her, and a flame of warmth licked its way into her awareness before she could look away.

"What do you mean, for you? They're naming him for both of us. At least that's what Tomas said—but then, he was suffering under a slight handicap this morning. I believe his head was about to fall off."

The tears that had been rising and sinking with tiresome regularity ever since Gardiner had shown up in the middle of the night threatened to overflow this time. Daisy took a deep breath and set out at a fast, if slightly stiff-legged, pace, with Gardiner right behind her.

"No kidding," he said cheerfully, "I think that's pretty fine, don't you? I've never had a baby named after me before."

She snorted. "Frankly, I don't know why they bothered. They probably just told you that out of politeness, knowing you'd never know the difference."

"That's all you know. Tomas and I hit it off pretty well, considering I wasn't feeling too great after sharing my sleeping quarters with the livestock—and you, of course—and he had a granddaddy of a hangover. You wanna know what I think? I think he kind of appreciated my coming after you, since it meant he wouldn't have to leave his family long enough to lead you back himself. Joaquin Gentry Mendoza. Has a ring to it, wouldn't you say?"

Daisy's legs were longer than Gardiner's, although he was a few inches taller. It didn't seem to matter. He had no trouble keeping up with her. "Yeah, it rings like a piece of broken dime-store crockery. Hayn-tree. Sounds like a cross between a health food and a storage closet."

Gardiner reached out and grabbed her by the shoulders, spinning her around to face him. "What's got you so riled this morning? Didn't you sleep well?"

"Nothing's got me riled! I'm just sore and itchy and I want to get back to my room. Do you mind?" She tried to break away, but he held her there.

"You want to let me clean you up a little first—make you halfway presentable before you go charging through the front lobby?"

"I can clean myself up, thanks, if you'll just let go of my arms?" *Damn, damn, damn, don't let me cry now! He'll think it has something to do with him, and it doesn't!*

"Sure you can, honey. It's just that knowing how you feel about people staring at you, I thought I'd sort of dust you off a little before we get there."

Her shoulders slumped and for an instant—the merest fraction of an instant—he held her against him. Then he set her away and carefully removed a stem of dried grass and several seeds from her hair.

"Oh, Lord, I probably look like a scarecrow," Daisy muttered, finger-combing her hair while Gardiner straightened her collar. She tried to brush out a few of the worst creases in her orange linen shorts while he tilted her face to the light, examining the bruise on her cheek. There were several scratches, as well, and one large pink mosquito bite, and to top it off, her nose was beginning to peel.

"Yeah, I guess you do at that." He touched her bruise with infinitely tender fingers. "This hurt?"

"Only when I smile."

"How about your knees?"

"Only when I walk."

"I reckon I could carry you, but you're so damned long, you'd probably hang off both ends and drag on the ground."

"Forget it. You're too old to be lifting weights."

"Honey, we're both long past it, as far as that goes, but I could probably manage to carry you if I had to."

Laughter danced in his eyes like sunshine on gray windswept waters. It was contagious, but Daisy didn't crack a smile. "That's so sweet, but you know your back isn't up to it. At your age—"

"What about yours? You're probably not all that much older than I am—even so, once a woman hits forty-five, she really oughtta start looking after herself a little better."

She giggled, and then winced as her facial abrasions protested. "Forty-five! I'm only thirty-eight, and I can prove it!" Four years ago, she'd considered herself almost too old at thirty-four to be starting over. Oddly enough, thirty-eight no longer seemed old at all. "Where did you develop your smooth technique with women, if you don't mind my asking?"

"Technique? Blossom, you flatter me." Gardiner's grin slowly faded. Even now he could recall a certain high-school cheerleader who had made it pretty plain that she was interested if he was. The first time he'd got up enough nerve to ask her out, after making his brothers swear a blood oath to be in bed by ten and to see that their old man didn't try to sneak a smoke, he'd stuttered so hard she'd laughed in his face. The next day, all the girls in school had giggled and whispered and cast him sly looks.

Funny—on the football field, he could call a play without missing a syllable. Even in Nam, the only time he'd had much trouble had been with a woman he'd met in Bangkok.

Technique, he thought as they slogged along the narrow trail, past a flowering bush covered with butterflies, past the area where he'd seen at least twenty vultures clinging to a dead tree, past the dump with the half-carved mahogany tree. He could count on one hand the women he'd slept with in his lifetime. There was only one whose name he could easily recall, and within a year or two, he'd probably have trouble remembering her.

Did that add up to technique? He'd never even thought about the subject before, much less tried to cultivate one. He wished to God he had—he could use an advantage about now. Only a few more days left, and suddenly Daisy Valentine was beginning to matter to him. Matter a whole hell of a lot.

The closer they came to the hotel, the more unreal the past twenty-four hours seemed to Daisy. By the time they had reached her door, she could have almost convinced herself none of it had happened. Almost.

Taking a deep breath, she arranged a smile on her face, turned and held out her hand, and Gardiner gripped it firmly. "Well…thanks for coming after me, friend. I could have probably found my way back alone, but I'm just as glad not to have had to try. Green swamps full of crawly animals aren't my favorite things."

"You would have made it just fine. There's a trail—it's just kind of hard to see unless the sun's at the right angle."

"We both know I'd have probably tripped over a jaguar and landed up to my ears in a swamp full of alligators."

He grinned, looking homely and handsome and achingly dear to her. "Iguanas, maybe. And you probably wouldn't have made it quite up to your ears. Except for a few cenotes, the swamps around here are mostly surface things."

Her hand was still resting in his, and it occurred to Daisy that the gesture was oddly formal considering that they had slept together the night before. And if circumstances had been slightly different, she was fairly certain that sleeping wasn't all they'd have done.

"He's a construction worker, you know."

"Who? What?"

"Tomas. He works construction, only at the moment he's laid off. And there are clinics available, only by the time he realized there was more to this birthing business than his mama had led him to believe, Josephina was in no shape to hike out to the highway and catch a ride."

"Oh." They were still clasping hands. It felt warm. It felt right. It felt explosive.

Daisy jerked her hand away and stuck it behind her back. "Yes, well . . . that's great. I mean that he has a . . . a profession. A trade, or whatever."

"I just didn't want you worried about the young Mendoza family. They'll make it. I'll keep track of them."

He was standing so close she could feel the warmth of him, smell the heady essence of sun-warmed skin and healthy masculine sweat. A warning buzzer went off in her head, shrill and demanding. She fumbled for her key. "Well, thanks, Gardiner—I mean, I won't. Worry, that is. And thanks again for . . ."

A moment later, she was leaning against the cool interior of her door, eyes closed, heart pounding. She'd been half an inch—half a *second* away from making a mistake that could make the fiasco with Beau look like an Easter-egg hunt.

Going through the motions of showering, of lathering her hair until her scalp ached, of smearing moisturizing cream on her bruises and the sunburn lotion on her insect bites—which probably wouldn't help much, but it was all she had—and climbing into her freshly made bed, Daisy steeled herself to face the problem and rationalize it away.

First off, she was dangerously close to falling in love with Gardiner Gentry. *Yeah, close! Like a tightrope walker is dangerously close to breaking his neck when he's leaning out at a forty-five-degree angle without a net.*

Secondly, it wasn't going to happen. Because she wasn't in the market for another disaster—not at this stage of her life. In three days she'd be going home, supposedly relaxed and rested after a wonderful vacation. Back to the land of reality, where life would consist of such sane and reasonable things as taking the yearly inventory, worrying about how to get the most bang for the shop's meager advertising bucks, placing next year's orders and trying to reach some sort of working agreement with the handful of temperamental craftsmen who were hell to deal with but too good to kiss off.

For creative satisfaction, there would be new displays to set up—she'd go back with a bundle of fresh new ideas. And for excitement, there would be a whole new slate of regional craft shows, where she could fight her way through the mobs on the off chance that she'd discover a single supplier with whom they could do business.

And on a more personal level? A fresh supply of books in the stores. New TV dinners at the grocer's that she hadn't even sampled yet. And don't forget, the networks usually tried out a new slate of programs this time of year. Laughing alone at dumb sitcoms wasn't so bad—it was better than not laughing at all.

As for the rest—the physical needs a woman her age was supposed to be at the peak of—there were always cold showers. She hadn't been overly impressed by what little she had known of passion. All the panting and pulsating and purple starbursts were a bunch of hype. She knew, because she'd been there.

Restlessly, she flopped over onto her stomach, as if she could avoid her own thoughts. All right, so she'd felt something dangerously close to starbursts with Gardiner. And panting and pulsating, too, for that matter. But for pity's sake, look at the circumstances! Moonlight in the jungle? Sleeping out under the stars with an attractive and virile man? Throw in an element of danger, the heart-wrenching emotion of helping a child be born, and there you have it—a surefire recipe for sexual hysteria if there ever was one.

Good Lord, if a woman could get all charged up from a simple handshake, what could she expect when she'd been lying bare-breasted on a narrow blanket, being kissed to within an inch of her life?

"Daisy?"

Oh, great. Now she was even hearing his voice. Flopping over onto her side, she yanked viciously at the gown that had twisted around her hips.

"Hey, Daisy, are you still awake?"

"Go away, damn you, you're spoiling my life," she muttered aloud, but too softly to be overheard.

"Daisy, the cleaning crew is in my room, and I can't get in. How about if I just come in and wash up in your bathroom, huh?"

"Gardiner, take a dive in the swimming pool, will you? I'm sound asleep."

"Good, then it won't bother you if I come in and use your space."

Furious—more because of the clamoring of her heart than the plaintive voice coming through her patio door, Daisy got out of bed and stalked across the cool tile floor.

She flipped the latch. "Just come in, do what you have to do, and get out again. I'm still asleep!"

"Your eyes are open."

Every pore in her body was open, breathing him in. "They are not," she snapped, squinting against the sliver of sunlight that poured in with him. She'd deliberately closed the louvres and the curtains to shut out the light. It was just a bit past ten-thirty, and she'd always had trouble sleeping during the day, but she was bushed.

A strange feeling of desperation swept over her. "All right! Wash. Shower. Brush your teeth. Do whatever you have to and then let yourself out quietly. The boys will be finished with your room by then.''

"The exterminators are waiting to get in next. After they're finished, I'm supposed to stay out for an hour or two at least."

"That's your problem, not mine."

"Okay, go back to bed. I promise, I won't bother you."

"Oh, good gravy," she muttered, and stomped back to fling herself down onto the king-size bed.

She was wide awake, of course. Over the hum of the ceiling fan, she listened to the shower, listened while he brushed his teeth, listened to the silence and imagined him scrunching his face this way and that, scraping off lather and bristles and then rinsing his razor, the way her father had done a hundred years ago, before he'd taken off for the Alaskan oil fields and a string of other women.

And then she felt the bed give on the far side. "Daisy?"

"Don't talk to me, you're supposed to be gone by now."

"I don't want to go."

Tired of the game they were playing—no, not tired; frightened—Daisy rolled over to confront him. He was wearing a pair of clean khakis and no shirt. His hair was wet, the gray temporarily hidden. A trickle of water dripped from the bush of dark silken hair under his arms.

He smelled like soap and toothpaste and something masculine and dangerously alien, and she knew beyond a shadow of a doubt that they were going to make love.

And that she wanted it more than she had ever wanted anything in her life.

Nine

—

"This has been coming on for a long time," Gardiner said hoarsely, his words muffled against her throat.

"I know." Daisy was past dissembling. What good had it done her? He had seen right through her hardshell pose, just as he'd seen through her pretense of indifference. She slipped her arms around his chest and stroked the satin-smooth muscles of his back. Angling downward toward his waist, her hand encountered a small patch of hair, and she combed through it with her fingers.

"You wanna t-t-talk first?"

"No." The less said, the better. She didn't want to think about what she was doing, much less talk about it—about how she was going to feel when they went their separate ways on Sunday.

"Luckily, the store was open." There was an edge to his voice that told her even more than the trembling strength of his muscles how much his control was costing him. "I—uh, have p-p-protection for you."

"Thank you, Gardiner. That was thoughtful."

"Yeah . . . Jeez, would you listen to us? Next thing, you'll be asking me if I'd like a cup of tea first."

They were lying near the edge of the bed—she'd rolled over toward him, not the other way around. Her arms were around his waist now, her head on his shoulder, and he was tracing a course from the base of her throat out and then down the inside of her arms with his fingertips. Who would ever have dreamed that there were a hundred erogenous zones between a woman's elbow and her collarbone?

"Are you trying to say you'd like to change your mind? I understand, Gardiner. It's no big deal, you know. I mean, circumstances and all—it's easy to get carried away, but that doesn't mean—"

He laid a finger over her lips, stopping the nervous flow of words. "Daisy, I don't want to call anything off. I just wish I weren't going to be leaving Saturday, but—"

"You mean Sunday."

His fingers trailed down her throat again, down over her collarbone, over her shoulder, tucking under her arm and then moving slowly down to ring her wrist. Each time he had done that, he'd brushed the sides of her breast, causing the air to jam in her lungs. "No, Saturday," he said quietly. "I was here a day ahead of you, remember?"

Daisy closed her eyes and attempted to deny the pain. "Too bad. We could have shared a cab to the airport,'' she quipped, her voice sounding surprisingly normal.

Why couldn't he have waited to tell her that when she was perched on a bar stool, sipping a mango daiquiri and wearing her white silks, her Panama hat and her chunkiest jewelry? She might have been able to handle it with a little panache then. Dammit, it just wasn't fair to wait until she was lying in bed with her arms wrapped around him—around this warm sweet hunk of a man who was determined to ruin everything she'd spent the past four years building up.

"Daisy? You okay down there?" He tried to pry her face out of his shoulder.

"Mmm-hmm," she murmured, not budging. Sure she was okay. Her face was naked as the day she'd been born. She'd creamed off the last smidgen of any remaining makeup—not so much as a hint of blusher colored her face. Her plain white cotton nightgown was rumpled around her hips, and going to bed with wet hair always made her look like Medusa. Oh, she was just fine.

No wonder he'd cooled down so fast.

"You want to know something funny, B-B-Blossom? I'm scared stiff."

She raised her head, her eyes widening on his. "You? I don't believe that, not for a minute."

"Why not? Did you think I was some kind of s-superstud or something?" He looked genuinely amazed.

What had she thought? The truth was, she hadn't—not since her first good look at him. Whichever part of her body had reacted so strongly, it certainly hadn't been her brain. "Do you think you'd be here in my bed if I thought you were a superstud?"

They were both lying on their backs now, and Daisy resettled her head on his shoulder. That way she didn't have to meet his eyes. After a moment in which neither of them spoke, Gardiner covered her clasped hands with one of his larger ones. It felt good. It felt . . . solid.

Just below his breastbone, where the flesh dropped off suddenly, she could see a rapid pulsing. She watched it, fascinated. Despite his calm voice and his seeming relaxation, his heart was going like a jackhammer. One swift glance below his belt was enough to reveal the most likely cause.

Daisy swallowed hard and closed her eyes, but not soon enough. He had been watching her. He knew exactly what she'd been looking at. He chuckled. "Yeah, well . . . I said I was scared, not dead."

"Of *me?*"

He rolled over to face her then, his breath warm against her face. "No, honey—of me. In case you hadn't noticed, I happen to be a middle-aged bachelor who's not much to look at, and while I don't claim to be a virgin, I'm not so experienced that I take these things for granted. I want to please you, but I'm a realist. There's always the possibility that I'll fail."

His voice was distinctly thready. Heaven only knew what that little confession had cost him in terms of ego and self-respect. Some woman must have really messed him up.

Daisy wanted to cry. Even more than that, she wanted to make love to him until he didn't know—or care—which end was up. She had slept with exactly two men in her life. Her pleasure had never been a priority with either one of them.

Turning onto her side, too, she parted her lips and placed her mouth over his hard chest, exploring with her tongue until she discovered the rigid point of his nipple. Following blind instinct, she bathed, nipped, kissed and caressed until she heard a raw groan emerge from somewhere deep inside his chest.

Power. Never before had she realized that power could be so wildly intoxicating. It was unbelievably stimulating—this taking charge, this knowing that a man wanted her. For once in her life she felt truly desirable. It was an incredibly heady sensation.

Trailing her fingertips down to his waist, she felt his hard flat midriff shudder under her touch. When she began to tug at his belt buckle, he let loose a short expletive between clenched teeth.

His hands came down over hers, but she pushed them away. "Let me—I want to. I want *you* Gardiner."

He drew her up over him with excruciating slowness, his hands biting into her flesh. "Easy, easy— you're t-t-tiptoeing through a m-m-minefield, sweetheart—I just hope you know what you're letting yourself in for."

Daisy tried to take the initiative in the kiss that followed, but she was no match for him. By turns plundering and seducing, he led her to the very edge and back again, over and over, his hard body throbbing fiercely against hers. Not until they were both totally breathless did he hold her away, his eyes scorching her like hot ice.

She was dazed, and probably looked it. He smiled at her then, making it infinitely worse. "Okay now, Daisy blossom, where were we when I interrupted you?"

And he placed her hands back on his buckle.

For a woman who had always professed to be good with her hands—at five, she'd excelled in finger painting, at fourteen, she could type eighty accurate words a minute, and the summer she was eighteen, she had learned to play a creditable claw-hammer banjo—Daisy botched it. The buckle was one of those male things that you had to be born with the Y chromosome to understand. She jammed the zipper, and then she was terrified that she'd pinch the part of him that was straining to be set free. The more her fingers raked against his hardened manhood, the more her hands shook.

And the more audible Gardiner's breathing grew. By the time she had succeeded in dragging his pants down over his hips, he was gasping for air.

"Are you laughing?" she asked with sudden suspicion. Sitting cross-legged, she tugged his khakis down the last few inches and flung them across the room in a clatter of keys, belt buckle and loose change.

"Believe me, I'm not laughing. Crying, maybe, but definitely not laughing." He sat up, his movement fluid, his body sleek and beautiful in the shadowy bedroom. If this was an example of a middle-aged man, Daisy thought, grinning, she pitied all those poor young jocks out strutting their stuff on the beach. They couldn't hold a candle to Gardiner Gentry. Literally.

"Your turn, Blossom." Taking the gown in both his hands, he peeled it off over her head. Instinctively, Daisy reached for the sheet to cover herself. Just as deliberately, Gardiner pulled it down again. He was smiling, almost as if he were relaxed—or as relaxed as a man could feel under those particular circumstances.

Taking his time, he gazed at her openly. "I think you're probably about the loveliest woman ever created," he said with a thoughtfulness that made Daisy almost believe him.

She stared at him, forgetting to breathe. He hadn't even tried to pretend that she was beautiful. He hadn't tried to tell her she was gorgeous. He'd called her lovely—*probably* lovely. Somehow, that was much better than if he'd flat out called her beautiful, which she wasn't. She was painfully aware, having been reminded more than a few times, of her too-square jaw, her graying hair, her small breasts, and her basketball player legs.

"Thank you, Gardiner."

Taking both her hands in his, he tugged her over until she fell on top of him, and then he captured her lips in a long sweet kiss. In her entire life, Daisy had never been so aware of her own body. Nerves from the top of her scalp to the soles of her feet came startlingly alive. Her racing heartbeat echoed in the tips of her breasts, at the base of her throat—between her thighs.

Buns. So that was the part of a man's body loosely referred to as buns. She could see why. They even felt delectable!

Pressing herself against him, she gloried in the quick responsiveness of his hard masculine strength. She wanted to touch him there, too—the way he was beginning to touch her. Gently, curiously, caressingly. Suddenly, she wanted desperately to feel his hard flesh leap under her fingers, wanted to hear the breath whistle through his teeth—wanted to make him whimper with need.

And then wanted to satisfy that need.

Her breath caught in her throat and she stiffened, her eyes widening in surprise. Those gentle fingers that had cupped her so sweetly just a moment ago, had begun to move again. Move with a touch so seductive, so compelling, that soon she was writhing, tightening her thighs, pushing at his hand.

"Let me, sweetheart. Let me do this for you," he whispered, and continued to work his magic until she was all but weeping.

As his relentless touch carried her further and further away from reality and closer and closer to the burning surface of the sun, she began to whimper. Until, drowning in a flood of unbelievably intense sensations, she clutched at him, trying to drag him over her body. "Gardiner, please... Oh, hurry, hurry," she whispered frantically.

Suddenly she stiffened, her thighs tightening on his hand. Her eyes were closed, her lips parted, and she cried softly. "Gardiner please... Gardiner, oh, darling, please..."

Only then, when he was satisfied that he could give her pleasure, did he move over her. Parting her thighs, he knelt between them and lifted her sleek long legs around his hips. So sweetly did she welcome him that he nearly lost control the moment he felt himself sink into her hot tight depths, but he held on, willing himself to give her time—time to catch up.

Together. More than anything in the world, he wanted them to come together in the truest sense of the word.

And they did....

Much later, Gardiner roused long enough to drag the sheet over them. Later still, Daisy opened her eyes long enough to reassure herself that she hadn't dreamed it— that he was still there, still holding her.

"Are you all right?" he asked.

"Mmm. Hungry, but other than that..."

He sighed and his arms tightened around her. "Next time, remind me to book us into a place that has room service."

"For that you'd need a telephone. I think the nearest one is in Cancun."

"Yeah, there's that little problem, too," he said, and then they were both quiet, because Daisy knew—and she knew that Gardiner knew, too—that there would be no next time. Not for them. He'd spelled it out pretty plainly—he'd be leaving on Saturday. End of chapter. End of story.

After a while, he said, "Daisy, I don't think there's a graceful way to say this, so I'll just say it right out."

Don't, she warned silently. I know as well as you do that there's no future in it—we both know the difference between like and lust and love.

"You don't have to say anything, Gardiner. I understand." She'd been toying with a twist of his hair— he had nice hair. Sort of warm chestnut, with gray. Thick. Lustrous. Virile.

"I can only say I'm sorry. But it might help if you knew that I had a physical before I came. A complete physical. A *very* complete physical. I'm okay." He didn't want her worried on that account. Just because she'd gone to bed with an old fool who bragged about buying protection and then forgot to take the damned thing out of the wrapper and use it, he didn't want her losing any sleep over it. "Like I said, I'm not real good at this seduction stuff. I forgot. Remembered to get it, but forgot to use it. I'm sorry as hell, honey."

Wheels spun as Daisy caught up with what he was telling her. "Oh. Well, if you need any reassurance, I suppose I'd better tell you that there hasn't been anyone since my husband. We've been divorced for four years, and even before that—ah . . . well, it's probably been at least five or six years for me."

He held her then, burying his face in her hair, stroking her back. It was more comforting this time than sexual—which was odd, Daisy thought distractedly, because it was exactly the way he'd held her and stroked her before, when he'd set her on fire.

She slipped her arms around him. "As for the other—I'm a little too old to be worrying about getting pregnant, so you're safe there, too."

His arms tightened around her. "I hate to be the one to burst your bubble, Daisy blossom, but thirty-eight isn't exactly over the hill. Look, I'll give you my card. If there are any, uh, repercussions, will you promise to get in touch with me?"

"There won't be. It's the wrong time of the month. But thanks, Gardiner." What would he have done? Offered to marry her? Offered her money for an abortion?

She had a brief soaring moment of euphoria picturing herself with a tiny paler version of little Joaquin

Tomas. It wouldn't happen, of course, but if by some fluke of nature it did...

She was still wallowing in a warm maternal glow when Gardiner's deep drawl cut through. "What happened with you and whatsisname? Why'd you split up, I mean?" He hooked a foot under her left ankle and eased her leg over his. It felt good. She left it there.

"Beau? He wasn't quite as optimistic about my potential as you are. By the time he got to where he was ready to start his family—that's what he called it...not *our* family, but *his* family—I was too old to be considered prime breeding stock."

Gardiner raised his head off the pillow and stared down at her. "You're not serious?"

"Yep. Beau liked to use statistics a lot. He quoted the odds on my chances of delivering a healthy baby and compared it with the odds of a twenty-one-year-old woman. There is a difference, you know. Marginal, but real enough when a man's looking for excuses. Besides, my mother was diabetic. She died in her early forties of a heart attack. Two more marks against me, in spite of the fact that my mother was five foot three and weighed 164 pounds."

"You took after your father, I gather. Is he still, ah..."

"Living? Probably. Somewhere. He took off when I was seven. Last I heard, he was working with an oil company in Alaska. All six foot four, 157 pounds of him."

"I take it your ex was genetically flawless?"

Daisy took a deep breath and expelled it. She didn't really want to talk about Beau and the babies she'd wanted to have and he hadn't—with her, at least. It no longer mattered. "I don't know. I never asked. He did have a quietly vicious way of cutting a person down to size—down to *his* size. But I don't think that's considered a genetic flaw."

There was a long silence during which Gardiner silently called Daisy's ex-husband some extremely unflattering names. For a math professor, his vocabulary was surprisingly creative, but then, in moments of stress, he was apt to revert to the coal mines of southern West Virginia. Or the killing fields of Southeastern Asia.

"Did you love him?" he asked after a while.

"When I married him? You know, to this day I'm not sure if it was love or just one of these zing-bam-pow crushes that usually hits when a girl's about fourteen. I was twenty-nine at the time. Beau was a twenty-one-year-old law student who looked and talked like a thirty-year-old seasoned politician. He was smooth and incredibly good-looking."

"And Daisy? What was she like back then?"

Daisy smiled a little wistfully. "Depressingly earnest, I'm afraid. I was a glorified gofer for a state senatorial candidate. His wife happened to be my second cousin, and when the company I worked for folded and I needed a job, she got me a place on her husband's office staff. I thought I was going to save the world by filling out forms in triplicate—I should have known better. I'm the world's worst form-filler-outer. God, we must have used up whole landfills!"

Gardiner chuckled, and Daisy snuggled closer, despite the steadily increasing heat in the room. It must be well past noon by now. Siesta time. "That was before I began to suspect that the true purpose of government is to appoint study committees, to generate paperwork, and to perpetuate itself. I was still pretty idealistic when I met Beau. He had political ambitions,'' she continued, ''but he had to finish law school first. Who better to help him than a working wife whose cousin was married to a three-termer with a lot of clout?''

''So what happened?''

''We had a big fancy wedding—Beau insisted on inviting every Democrat in the House and Senate. I was still paying for it when we broke up. Meanwhile, Cousin Claude and his clout got defeated, Beau flunked out of law school and walked straight into one of those positions made to order for men like him—the kind where the biggest airhead always rises to the top.''

''And Daisy Valentine, what about her?''

''Daisy Monclare. Oh, she turned into a dowdy housewife—sweats, sneakers and good works. Like I said, depressingly earnest. Meanwhile, Beau met another lady who wasn't quite so earnest. Several of them, in fact, but this one in particular. She had everything I lacked. Looks, money, background, big boobs and even bigger contacts.''

When he didn't say anything, Daisy lifted her head to steal a glance. He was smiling. No, he was grinning. Irritably, she demanded to know what as so funny.

''Just trying to picture you as a dowdy housewife. The sweats and sneakers I can handle, but not the dowdy part. Not in a million years.''

She relaxed again. ''D'you ever study those makeover pictures in the women's magazines?''

''Can't say that I have.''

"Take my word for it—I was the perfect 'before.' Shapeless hair—too busy saving the world to take time for a decent cut. No time to put on makeup—who needed it? A smear of moisturizer, a daub of lipbalm and I was set for the day. At that time I was working with a group that was trying to convince the city that some of the empty office buildings and vacant stores would make dandy shelters for the homeless. Leading a bunch of architects, businessmen and politicians through deserted buildings didn't require a whole lot in the way of a wardrobe. A hard hat and steel-toed shoes would have been more practical."

"What did your husband think?"

She shrugged, and his arm tightened around her shoulders. "On paper it sounded fine. 'Mrs. Beau Monclare, wife of prominent local business executive, heads committee to blah-blah-blah. Daisy Monclare organizes retirement-home rocking squad to work with addicted newborns.' Oh, yeah, Beau liked it just fine. No reason not to—it was good PR for an ambitious young businessman, and besides, it kept me busy while he organized his own little fun and games."

"Daisy..."

"What?" she muttered, embarrassed at having dragged out the old Daisy and introduced her to a man she wanted to impress. It was just that same stupid streak that had kept her from tinting the gray in her hair. She couldn't hide the real Daisy Valentine—not with anyone who mattered. It would be like lying.

"Monclare was a brainless jerk."

"Mmm-hmm."

He hooked her right leg with his foot, reached down and dragged it up over his thigh, along with her left one. She was practically lying across his lap now.

"Daisy?"

"Hmm?"

"Thanks for telling me."

"Mmm-hmm."

He began toying with her left breast, sliding his palm around to the side and cuddling it up into a small heap, then running his thumb over the top.

"Daisy?" he said again, his voice slightly huskier than before.

"Hmm?" It was more a sigh than a response.

"I was always taught never to waste anything. Actually, it never came up—there was never anything left over to waste."

Daisy turned to look into his face, wanting to know about him—wanting to know everything that made Gardiner Gentry the special man he was.

"I bought this thing—you know, the whatchamacallit—before I came over here to your room? And I, uh, sure hate to waste it."

It took her a moment to follow his meaning. When she did, she dissolved into laughter, and he chuckled along with her. And then she was no longer on his lap, but straddling him, and he was running his hands—his wide sensitive powerful hands—up her sides and back down over her hips, his eyes closed, his lips slightly parted, the bony planes of his face standing out in sharp relief.

"And if I don't get into the damned thing right now, we're going to end up wasting it again," he grated.

She had never had occasion to use one before. Beau had expected her to be responsible for birth control when they'd been married. He took it for granted that it was a woman's duty, and so naturally, she had, too.

Now she insisted on helping, and her help nearly sent them both over the edge. Laughing, Gardiner lifted her up and then eased her back down until he was tightly sheathed in her warmth.

The first time had been unbelievably good. Daisy had understood then what all the hoopla was about. This time, it was even better. There was time to give, time to build, time for Daisy to gaze down at Gardiner's face, loving him so—loving all that they were together.

When they finally collapsed in a damp panting heap, she said, "I'm glad I didn't know you when you were younger. I don't think I could have stood it."

He stroked her hair back from her face and brushed kisses on her eyebrows, and then on her scratches and her bruised cheek. "Funny—I was just thinking, I wish I'd met you about twenty years ago. Make that fifteen. Twenty years ago, I wouldn't have been in any position to take advantage of you." Twenty years ago he'd been fresh out of the army and trying without much success to hold his family together.

"Twenty years ago," Daisy said softly, "I was eighteen, studying art, working two jobs, trying to learn to play my grandfather's banjo and taking a business course at night. I was better at the banjo than at business, and that's not saying much."

"Manual dexterity?"

"Exactly. Fastest two fingers in the East. Unfortunately, I had a tin ear."

"At least you had the guts and imagination to try. Still do. It shows—even the tin ear." He grinned, and Daisy thought of the outrageous earrings she favored.

"Rusty tin. Hmm, it's a thought. The color would look great with turquoise—or maybe onyx."

"See? What'd I tell you? Guts and imagination."

"And inflamed ears. What about you, Gardiner? What were you like twenty years ago?" *What are you like now? Why do I feel as if I've known you forever?*

"Dull. Not worth mentioning."

"You couldn't be dull if you took a graduate course in it," she said flatly. If he saw himself that way now, it was because someone—a woman, probably—had convinced him that it was true. Daisy hated the thought of any woman's having that much power over Gardiner Gentry. "Gardiner, what were you doing then—"

He didn't let her finish. "What do you say we grab a shower, see what we can round up in the way of supplies and hit the beach? I'd kind of like to check out that shipwreck one last time, wouldn't you?"

She'd kind of like to know what he'd been doing and what he'd been like twenty years ago. And thirty. And one. However, even Daisy knew enough to sense when a man didn't want to talk about something. She decided not to push it. "Sounds good to me. You want to go first or shall I?"

Together, she wanted him to say. From now on, we do everything together!

"I expect my room's inhabitable by now. Why don't I just run upstairs, shower and dress and come back for you in, say, fifteen minutes? Half an hour?"

She hid her disappointment. Sitting up, she struck a pose, forking her hair back with her fingers. "Take your time, I'm only slightly famished. I'll go ahead and see what I can pry out of the bartender. He's got to have leftover *something,* even if lunch ended hours ago.''

''That's the plan, then. First one dressed will raid the bar. Make mine tacos and beer—two orders of each, to go.''

''Sure. And if you get there first, make mine a double cheeseburger with bacon and fried onions. And a double chocolate shake. With fries on the side—a double order. And catsup, not that stuff with the peppers in it, okay?''

''Impossible,'' he said. ''Which translates loosely to fat chance.''

Laughing, Daisy attempted to get up, but he caught her and dragged her back against him, kissing whatever was within reach—her neck, her nape, her shoulder blade.

Then he said, ''Remind me to stop by the store again if it's open, hmm?''

Ten

___

By the time Daisy spread the beach towel for their impromptu picnic, the sun had settled behind a bank of lavender clouds. Just above it, a flock of smaller clouds, like so many pink sheep, drifted aimlessly across a field of pale turquoise, while higher still, the color darkened to purest cobalt.

"I can't believe this is the same sky we have back home," she said, leaning against a rocky outcropping that still held the sun's warmth.

"There's a physical reason why it looks different," Gardiner said, "but I doubt that you're wanting to hear it."

"If you mean the fact that this is a film set for a Bo Derek movie, and Petersburg, Virginia, is the real world, I already knew that." Carefully, she smoothed a patch of sand with one hand.

When he failed to comment for several moments, she glanced up. He was seated at the other end of the towel staring out across the water, his back half-turned toward her. In a pair of faded khakis, his white shirt pressed against his body by the light breeze and his tanned and rugged profile in bold relief against the exotic tropical sunset, he was obviously a part of the film set, not the real world.

Sighing, Daisy began to draw patterns in the sand. Circles intertwined with still more circles. Chains. It was time she began pulling back—she had her work waiting for her. One shop now, maybe another one later on. A chain of Daisy Chains—that was something to look forward to, wasn't it?

And Gardiner—next week this time, he'd be back in his classroom. Mexico would seem like a dream, and be forgotten just as quickly. All of it. From the looks of him, he'd already forgotten her.

"Penny for them?" he said just as her fingers closed over something smooth and round.

Stroking the pebble, she said, "Oh . . . nothing very earthshaking. Just thinking about getting back to work." Just wondering what *he'd* been thinking about while he was staring out over the water with that intent look on his face. Caribbean resorts weren't exactly geared for intense thoughts. "What about you?"

Shrugging, he reached for the basket of food. "Work. Yeah, getting back, easing into the rut again. I'm not sure this kind of vacation was such a great idea."

She waited until he'd dealt out the sandwiches and set out the plate of cheese and fruit before she asked why not.

"Why not? I don't know... Maybe because it makes everything seem too easy. Santa Claus, Easter Bunny—the whole works. A guy could get used to living this way and never want to go back."

"Hmm, I know what you mean." Daisy took a big bite of her sandwich and poked back the oil-and-pepper-drenched grilled chicken and salad that threatened to slide out from between the slabs of coarse bread. "Caribbean Lotusland 101, prerequisite to Drop Out 201," she said when she could speak again.

She wanted to think she was a part of that eternal present he hated so much to leave. Even more than that, she wanted to believe that she could be a part of his future.

No, she didn't. She had her own future all mapped out, and it definitely did *not* include getting involved with another man. After four years and a lot of struggles, she had managed to regain control of her life. She finally had her act together, and the only way she could keep it that way was to avoid temptation like the measles.

Meanwhile, there on the other end of her beach towel, frowning at a leaky chicken sandwich, sat temptation personified. Neon warning signs had been flickering in her head since the first time she'd laid eyes on the man. *Remember Beau, remember Beau, remember Beau!*

The last time she'd gotten seriously involved with a man, she'd been lucky enough to walk away—all right, so she'd limped away, but at least she'd escaped. And lived to tell the tale.

She was older now—not quite so resilient, but considerably smarter. One of the things she had learned was the difference between a superficial wound and a fatal one. Getting over Beau had been bad enough. Getting over Gardiner would be devastating. Because there was nothing at all superficial about Gardiner Gentry.

"So," she said with breezy impersonality. "What made you pick a place like Club Caribe Azul for a vacation?"

Gardiner opened the bottle of chilled wine and poured it into the two stemmed globes provided by the bar. "I didn't. A—a friend wanted to come here, and I went along. She dropped out, so I came alone."

"She?" Daisy couldn't have been more shocked if he'd kicked her.

Brows flattened over his steely eyes, he said, "Yes, *she*. She was a college girl half my age, and we were engaged for a few weeks. At least, I thought we were. She had other ideas, so we split, but you can save your sympathy—I am *not* brokenhearted, I am *not* on the rebound—and incidentally, you don't have to tell me I should be old enough to know better because I do!" He scowled at the glorious sunset and muttered into his collar, "At least I do now."

Daisy hadn't been about to tell him anything. Once she got over her initial shock, she felt like kicking something big and solid. She felt like throwing something—preferably at him. But there wasn't one damned thing she wanted to say to him—at least nothing she had any right to say.

"Enough about ancient history. Tell me about this business of yours."

She covered her feelings well, having had years of practice. "Oh, um, the shop? It's small—just a small nook in a small shopping center, but we're proud of it. We sell handmade accessories, mostly jewelry. After nearly four years, we've built up a stable of excellent craftsmen to supply us and a pretty good clientele.''

''You started it from scratch?''

''With a partner—she's the brains, I'm the brawn, and I could talk about it all day, but unless you're interested in retailing or crafts, you'd be bored stiff.'' And the new Daisy Valentine was not boring. Gaudy, arrogant, outrageous, perhaps, but never boring. ''What I want to know is what made you get interested in math? What was it like growing up in a family of five boys?'' There—that wasn't too personal, was it? Nothing a game-show host wouldn't ask a contestant.

Gardiner didn't want to talk—not about himself. It would be like opening a door, and he had a sinking feeling that once she got her foot in the door, he would never be able to close it again. It might already be too late, but he was going to try. For both their sakes, he was going to give it his best shot.

''Who knows why anyone gets interested in anything?'' *You know why you got interested in her, man—because you couldn't even watch her sneeze without getting so damned turned on you had to prop a book over your lap!* ''Just the way a particular brain twists and turns, I suppose. I could ask what got you interested in selling jewelry?''

''No fair—it's still your turn. What about your family?''

''Boys. Five of 'em. I told you that, didn't I?''

''I was an only child. What was it like growing up with four brothers?''

Gardiner grimaced. He took another bite of his sandwich, wrapped the other half and stuck it back into the basket. He didn't want to think about the past—he didn't want to talk about it. And he especially didn't want to talk about it to her.

"Oh, what you'd expect, I guess," he said. "Basketball hoop on one side of the house, permanently dented siding on the other from having too many baseballs pitched against it."

"What kind of house was it? We always lived in apartments, but I always wanted a house."

What kind of a house was it? Gray. Drab. Cold. Uninviting. "You know the old cliché about being too poor to paint, too proud to whitewash? I guess that would sum it up. Strictly a no-frills affair." No frills, no curtains, no rugs—no softening touches of any kind after his mother had died. They'd worn out, or gotten too filthy, and had been hauled off and never replaced. The house had always echoed. He'd hated that.

"You were the oldest?"

"Yeah." He'd been mother, father, truant officer, chief cook and bottle washer. Mostly he'd been too busy to resent it. The resentment had been there, though, simmering underneath. He still felt guilty as hell about that, but there wasn't much he could do about it now. He liked to think none of them had ever known how much he resented having to put his own life on hold from the time he was fourteen to nurse the old man and look after them. They had been too young to notice things like that, and he'd been pretty good at hiding his feelings—even from himself.

By the time Billy had been old enough to take over some of the responsibilities, the old man had been dead nearly three years and Gardiner had decided to join the army, more for selfish reasons than out of any great burning patriotism.

Someone in the family was going to have to get an education, and none of the others seemed particularly interested. It had been all he could do to keep them from dropping out. The mines were shutting down right and left—jobs were damned hard to come by. Especially jobs that would support, not to mention educate, five young hellions between the ages of thirteen and eighteen.

Gardiner had gone in the army with the express intention of getting some kind of training, plus a head start on an education that could get them all out of the coal mines. Somehow, he'd ended up in Vietnam, instead. And Billy had followed him in.

By the time Gardiner got home, Jeff had married Elloree James, the house had a new room built onto the back, a fresh coat of paint on the front, a few scraggly flowers and a lawn of sorts. There were curtains on the windows and rugs on the floors, and more importantly, there were decent meals on the table. Elloree was still a kid, herself—and pregnant at that—but she'd grown up in a big family and was perfectly capable of taking on her husband's brothers.

After a private session with each of the boys, Gardiner had turned over to Elloree practically every cent he possessed, promising to send more when he could spare it. Next he'd paid a visit to the cemetery where his parents were buried, and then he'd headed for the highway to hitch a ride out of town. It was time to get started on his own life.

Crazy thing was, he'd missed it; missed the close-ness of living with five rowdy males in a four-room house—six when his father had been alive. Missed the squabbles over whose turn it was to operate the old wringer-washer on the back porch, whose turn it was to cook the beans and cabbage, who was wearing whose clean shirt, and who was going to get to use the truck on his date.

Now, staring out at the brilliantly colored water, Gardiner wondered what he could have done differently to make things turn out better than they had. He wondered what the hell he was doing here in a place like this. He didn't belong here, any more than he had belonged with a beautiful kid like Georgia.

And while she was definitely no kid, he also had no business getting involved with a woman like Daisy Valentine. He'd never had the time or opportunity to learn to share his life with a woman, and it was too late to start now.

Unable to help himself, he stole a look at her. The sunset's glow had softened the fan of tiny lines at the corners of her eyes, diffused the unabashed gray in her hair. She could easily have passed for twenty-five. Would she want to hear that? Should he tell her?

He was suddenly scared stiff of saying the wrong thing. With Georgia, it had been no problem. She'd demanded compliments, pulling them out of him the same way she'd pulled gifts and concessions out of him—by expecting them. By demanding them. By pouting when she didn't get them, and making him feel like a selfish insensitive clod.

But Daisy was different. Daisy was more beautiful than Georgia would ever be, and it had nothing to do with features and figures. With all her splashy clothes and her attempts at arrogance, there was an innate sweetness and honesty about Daisy Valentine that drew him to her even more than her physical beauty—and God knows, that alone was enough to tie him in knots!

It was time to start winding down what had happened between them. Gardiner knew it. Just as he knew he wasn't going to do it. Not yet. He'd told her earlier that day that he was a frugal man because he'd grown up with too little to waste. And he knew he wasn't going to waste what little time remained.

They were both old enough to know the score. They'd gone into this thing knowing there was no future in it—a man who'd been single for forty-one years was no great prospect for marriage. And a woman who'd tried it once, failed, and been hurt badly at that failure, wasn't about to risk it again.

On the other hand, Gardiner rationalized, they were both intelligent enough to enjoy a brief mutually satisfying affair without making too much of it. That settled in his mind, he reached for the bottle and poured them both another glass of wine.

Daisy scowled at the circles she'd drawn in the sand. What the dickens was going on behind those steely gray eyes? He was hiding something, and there wasn't one blessed blooming thing she could do about it. If she pried, he'd clam up—he wasn't a garrulous man at the best of times. She almost wished he were—then she could have dismissed him. Chattering men had always turned her off. Enigmatic ones had always intrigued her.

Dammit, why wouldn't he talk?

Most of what she knew about him she'd learned from observation. For instance, he might teach school now, but he was no stranger to hard labor. The bones were too close to the skin on the palms of his hands. Beau had had soft hands. Gardiner's hands were hard. They were strong. They were exquisitely sensitive.

And she'd better get her mind off those hard, strong, exquisitely sensitive hands and just what they were capable of doing to a woman's body before she found herself in deep, deep trouble.

Think about his mind, Daisy. He's left brain, you're definitely right brain. No match there.

But what about that sense of humor that dovetailed so neatly with her own?

None of this dovetailing business, either—you know the rules!

All right, so the man had a functioning brain, a sense of humor, tons of character and integrity. What was so sexy about all that?

Everything. Just everything.

The flat-out truth was that there wasn't a cell in his body that wasn't sexy, and if she had her way, men like Gardiner Gentry would be forced by law to wear a warning sign stamped plainly on their flank in red ink saying This Is Prime Stuff. Too Rich for Your Blood, Lady!

For all the good it would do.

Rolling the pebble between the fingers of one hand, she fastened a brilliant smile on her face and reached for her glass. "If I didn't know better, I'd say this was hard cider and not wine."

Lazily reaching across the towel, Gardiner lifted the dripping bottle, scanned the label and then replaced it in the ice bucket. "*Manzana d'oro*. Means golden apple. You've been hitting the Berlitz again, haven't you?"

Laughter gurgled in her throat. "Honestly? Can they do that? Bottle cider as wine, I mean?"

"I thought cider was kind of thick. As long as we can see through it, I guess we'll both survive." He held up his glass and wiped off the beading, then peered into its golden depths. A distorted version of his eyes caught hers and held them for what seemed an eternity.

Daisy held her breath without realizing it. He was telling her something silently—telling her something she didn't want to hear. That he'd leveled with her from the first? That he wasn't interested in anything more than a holiday fling?

That much she already knew. At least her head knew it. Her heart seemed to be a slow learner. A couple of more days, her head reminded her heart—one more day, in fact—and it would be over. They would each go their separate ways with a lovely suntan and a few nice memories, and after a while, both would have faded and been forgotten.

"Here," she said, dropping the pebble she'd been toying with in his lap. "Something to remember me by. Want to take a quick swim before it gets too dark? Come on, last one in's a deviled egg!"

Daisy huddled in her window seat and stared out over the wing, fighting another bout of melancholy. It was the only word she could think of that could begin to describe what she was feeling—what she'd been feeling ever since Gardiner had left her bed sometime before dawn the day before to catch the first flight out of Cancun.

Resentment, hatred, anger—she'd tried them all. Actually, she'd felt them all for a while, but the dregs were pure melancholy. Her last day had been wasted in trying to decide whether or not to try to hand-wash her bag of laundry and thinking about the night before.

They had gone for a swim, had raced, in fact. Her form had been better than his, but he'd won easily, his powerful stroke propelling him through the water like a seal. Laughing, they'd come out, dried off and devoured the rest of the food before going back to the hotel.

By the time they had showered and changed, they'd both been starved again, and they'd headed for the dining room, heaping their plates and going back for more.

"Where do you store it?" he'd asked, grinning as he watched her pack away her third dessert.

"In my feet," she'd told him gravely.

"By the way, did you ever get the spur out, or whatever was in there?"

Daisy had nodded, leaning back and wishing she could unbutton her waistband. "Once I gave up trying to operate blind and got out my reading glasses, it was a cinch."

"Reading glasses? I've never seen you wearing them. No wonder you have trouble using that little book of yours."

"I don't have trouble *using* it—I only have trouble *reading* it. There's a subtle difference there, Gentry."

"Too subtle. It escapes me completely."

"Put on your own glasses if you can't see it," she said, eyes dancing in a solemn face.

They'd walked out onto the pier and stood for a while, not touching, each acutely aware of the other. Aware that it was coming to an end. In silent agreement, they had turned and walked back to Daisy's room, where they sat out on the patio listening to the canned music, the laughter of the group that gathered nightly at the bar and those who gathered around the pool for whatever game the rec director had dreamed up for the night's entertainment.

"Do you want me to go back to my room?" Gardiner had asked after a while.

She didn't even have to think about it. "Please stay."

And he had. Stayed and made love to her again and again. The first time they had come together it had been slow, almost deliberate. As if both were thinking that it was time to wind up their brief affair, wondering how they could.

He had been sweet, tender, asking her what pleased her, and then, when she'd been too shy to tell him, leading her on with a skill that had come from some source she could only guess at.

From caring, she'd wanted to believe, but hadn't quite dared. He did care for her, of course. Only not enough.

Daisy knew that she had far exceeded the boundaries of her own limited experience that last night together, making him gasp and moan with pleasure. Making him tremble and close his eyes while every muscle and tendon in his body responded to her touch. And she'd delighted in it, because no matter how petty it was, no matter how selfish, she wanted him to remember her long after she had succeeded in putting him from her mind.

As if she ever could.

Just before daylight they had both awakened, hot and needy, and come together with an urgency that had been almost shocking in its intensity.

"I was dreaming about you," Gardiner had said by way of explanation when he could speak again.

"I must have been dreaming, too," Daisy had confessed. "I don't remember." That was a lie. She'd remembered, all right. And now she was wondering how she was going to manage to forget.

Daisy put the final touch on the display and stepped outside into the empty mall to study the effect. She had started the minute the shop had closed at five and worked steadily for the next seven and a half hours, pausing only to share a cup of coffee with the security guard.

She must be tired. Oversaturated with Mexicana. How could she expect to see the blooming thing with any degree of objectivity when she'd been going flat out for eighteen hours a day ever since she'd arrived home exactly a week ago today?

She would know tomorrow. If Cora Joan walked in, flipped the sign on the door, opened the register and didn't say one word about the new display, then she'd know it was a dismal flop. Cora didn't mince words. She might withhold them on occasion out of kindness, but when she used them, she did so with an accuracy any self-respecting gunslinger would have envied.

Hitching up her rumpled linen slacks, Daisy plopped down on the step stool. Come to think of it, her friend and business partner didn't always withhold unfavorable judgments, either. For instance, she had left Daisy in no doubt of her opinion when she'd met her at the airport a week ago.

"I told you not to drink the water," she'd said.

"What water? Have I missed something here?" Busy reclaiming her luggage after a tiresome, twice-delayed flight, Daisy was in no mood for cryptic remarks.

"You look worse now than you did when you left. You looked like hell then. Now you look like—"

"Thanks. I really needed that. How's it going? Did that stuff from Eloise ever come in?" All it had taken was the cold drizzle, the sound of Cora Joan's tart tongue, and she was back home again. Back to the real world.

It had been a vast relief to know that she'd left all that unsettling business with Gardiner somewhere in the land of palm trees and turquoise waters. Lugging her bags out to the car while her friend filled her in on daily averages and minor crises, she had congratulated herself on having put her world back into proper perspective.

She might have known it wasn't going to be that easy. Unpacking had been the first clue. Every sandy, salty item had brought back a hoard of painful memories. The bathing suit she'd worn when he'd kissed her underwater and run his hands inside the bra, lifting a breast out to suckle her nipple.

They'd both nearly drowned before he had finished with her—and then, of course, she'd had to repay him in kind.

There was the long orange, magenta and purple sheer sarong she'd worn the night before he'd left. They'd taken their dinner out under the stars, and then walked arm in arm, out to the pier, the warmth between their bodies increasing until they'd both been almost too aroused to make it back to the room.

She'd cried afterward, and then sworn she had a grain of sand in her eye. And he had pretended to believe her.

And then there were the pictures they'd taken with a borrowed Polaroid when they'd bicycled back to see the Mendozas one last time. There was one of Josephina and Tomas holding little J.T., and another of Daisy sitting cross-legged on a stump in front of the pig pen, her head bent over as she made pig noises for him.

"I think you've really got that little spotted one interested, honey," Gardiner had said, laughing.

"I'm trying to get J.T. to smile for the camera. He tried saying cheese, but *queso* just doesn't do it."

"I hate to tell you this, but babies that age don't smile. It's a documented fact."

She'd told him what she thought of his documented fact and gone on with her noises, tickling J.T.'s tiny chin with her finger. He'd continued to stare up at her with those enormous black eyes, and she'd felt her own tearing up. Just when she'd looked up to tell Gardiner to forget the pictures, he had started shooting.

There was the one of Gardiner and Daisy together, holding the baby. If she'd been smart, she'd have burned the thing. Instead, she'd spent hours this past week staring at it, touching it—as if somehow, she could reach through the glossy surface and touch Gardiner himself.

"Enough, already," she muttered. Dragging herself off the step stool, she began putting away the unused props, the hammer, tacks, tape and other paraphernalia she'd used to put together her Mexican vacation window.

It had been that way ever since she'd got home. Ever since she'd left Mexico. In fact, ever since Gardiner had left, the day before she had. She hadn't been able to keep her mind on the right track for more than ten minutes at a time without drifting back to things best forgotten.

At least she would sleep tonight. That alone was worth a few million pesos. And if she was very, *very* lucky, she wouldn't even dream.

"Ready to lock up, Miz Valentine?"

She spared a smile for the gray-haired security guard. They'd been friends ever since the first time she had locked herself in and her keys out four years ago. Her glitzy facade hadn't fooled Leonard Gilmer for a minute—he'd recognized her inexperience and insecurity and responded to it with a clumsy tact that had endeared him to her forever.

"Twelve-thirty. I'd say it's about time, Leonard, wouldn't you?"

"I'll walk you out to the parking lot."

It *couldn't* be seven o'clock! She'd just closed her eyes. Battling her way out from under layers of covers, Daisy squinted at the clock, tried to remember whether or not she'd told Cora Joan she wouldn't be in until noon, and decided it didn't matter. Cora Joan would open at ten, Donna would be in at one—between them they could handle it. They had managed for the two weeks she'd been in Mex—

Her eyes popped open. She scowled at the clock accusingly, but it was silent. She'd evidently shut it off the first time it had dared let out a *brrinng*.

The phone? The doorbell. What time was it, anyway?

"All right, all right, keep your pants on," she muttered, too groggy even to wonder who would be ringing her bell at this time of day.

She swung open the door and scowled at the man in the trench coat.

"I'm sorry," he muttered into his collar. "I should have called first. I'll go back to the motel and call now." He had actually turned away when Daisy came to her senses.

"Gardiner. *Gardiner?*" He turned, and Daisy would have given what was left of her life's savings to have been able to decipher his expression at that moment.

"This is a bad time, huh?"

"But what are you—no, it's not a bad time. I mean, what are you doing here, Gardiner?"

"Would you believe I just happened to be in the neighborhood and thought I'd drop by to see if you got home okay?"

Like a dunce, she nodded. She was still clinging to the front door. The cold late-January wind whistled past her bare legs unnoticed as her eyes continued to devour him.

"If you do, you're a sitting duck for every con man in the northern hemisphere."

He'd lost weight. He was wearing a beige trench coat and no hat, and his face was still tanned, but his cheekbones were more pronounced, his jaw just a bit more angular, and his eyes looked positively sunken.

"Do you think I could come inside? I mean, it's your heating bill—if you'd rather we stood here like this…"

Swinging the door wider, Daisy grabbed his arm and pulled him inside. They stared at each other for an interminable length of time, and then both began to speak at once.

"Gardiner, I've been—"

"Daisy, I couldn't—"

"You go first," she said, wrapping her arms around her shivering body. She hadn't turned up the furnace yet, nor had she taken time to put on her bathrobe. Another prime example of the way she'd been behaving since she got back. Like a guppy with the fantods.

"You want to get dressed?" Gardiner couldn't seem to stop looking at her legs—not surprising, since they constituted such a large part of her body. All the same, he was a serious man and he'd come to her with a serious purpose, and seeing her after what seemed a century, dressed in that same black-and-white shirt she'd worn on the beach back in Mexico, had hit him so hard he was practically catatonic.

It was a damned good thing he was wearing a topcoat. A pair of iron-reinforced briefs might be even better!

"Why don't I start the coffee and get something on? You— Uh, would you like to come in and sit down? Through here. The green chair's the most— Oh, and your coat. You can hang it in the closet if you— No, maybe I'd better. Stuff falls out."

She was practically wringing her hands. Gardiner couldn't stand it a second longer—the not knowing.

Grabbing her by the shoulders, he swung her around to face him. "Listen, Daisy—if you want me to go, I will. No questions asked. But I'll be back. You may as well get used to the idea, because I'm going to keep on coming back until you hear me out."

"Gardiner, I'm not—" She tried to break in, but he wouldn't let her. It was almost as if he were afraid to let her speak.

"No, don't say it. Give me a chance first. Look, you may as well know that I'm no expert on this business of courting a woman—I mean the way a man goes about it when he's dead serious. I'm probably doing it all wrong, but—"

Again she tried to interrupt, only to have him place a thumb gently over her lips.

"Flowers. I should have brought you some flowers. Or maybe you'd have preferred candy. Oh, hell—both. I'll get 'em later, okay? Jewelry, too—I know all women like jewelry. Only you probably know more about that than I do. Look, I just want you to know that whatever you want, I'll get it for you. I'm not a rich man, but I can afford to court you in style, only I don't know what kind of style you want. So if you'd just tell me—"

"You mean you're actually going to let me say something?"

He blinked at that, his stainless-steel eyes looking soft and caring and not at all cold. "Well...sure. Haven't I been trying to get you to tell me whether or not I stand a chance?"

"Give me your coat."

He did. He was wearing a suit, and he looked very different from the man she'd met on a palm-lined beach some twelve hundred miles away. He'd had a haircut, for one thing.

For another thing, this was the real world.

Daisy nudged the thermostat, waved toward the kitchen and said, "Do you know how to make coffee?"

"I make great coffee. I also make excellent toast, given the proper equipment."

"Then do something in there. I'm going to shower and get dressed, and then we'll talk."

She needed time to think. Her heart was going a mile a minute, but she took pride in not having thrown herself in his arms the minute she'd opened her front door.

Or rather, the minute she'd realized that she wasn't dreaming again—that Gardiner Gentry was actually right there within touching distance.

"So... what do you think?" Gardiner asked finally. He'd made coffee and toast, fried bacon and eggs, and rummaged around in her refrigerator, dragging out a tub of no-cholesterol margarine and three half-empty jars of orange marmalade.

Neither of them had eaten more than a few bites of anything.

"About what?" she countered.

"About what I said."

"Was that about the flowers, the candy, the jewelry, or making good coffee? You do, you know—this is better than mine."

He rose and stalked to the window, staring out at the wet school playground across the street. "I meant about courting you. If you're not interested, all you have to do is tell me." He sounded bitter, almost as if she'd already turned him down.

Sliding out of her chair, Daisy came to stand behind him. Telling herself she had nothing to lose and everything to gain, she wrapped her arms around his waist and rested her cheek on his back. She could feel him tense, hear the breath whistling in through his teeth.

"Daisy?" he said softly. "You'd better be sure—you'd better be damned sure, because I'm not going to give you a second chance to back out."

"Why did you come here, Gardiner?" She knew. She *almost* knew—but she still needed the words.

He turned then and gathered her in his arms, crushing her against him. Daisy buried her face in his throat and filled her senses with his familiar scent. Under the distinctive aroma of good woolens and freshly laundered cotton, it was just the same. The essence of Gardiner Gentry. The man she loved with all her heart and soul. "Why did you come here?" she repeated.

"Don't you know? Was it the same for you? God, I hope it was, sweetheart, because if I was wrong—if what we had wasn't real for you—then I'm not sure I can ever put the pieces back together."

"I love you."

He stopped breathing. And then his arms tightened and his lips found hers, and without a single word, he proceeded to tell her all that was in his heart.

A long time later, lying in her rumpled bed, they talked about tenure and a certain farmhouse in Wake County. They speculated on expanding her business to another state versus selling out entirely and starting over. They talked about families and hoped it wasn't too late to start one.

"But even if it is, we both know there's a little boy in the state of Quintana Roo with the name of Joaquin Tomas Daisy Gentry—"

"That's pronounced Hayn-tree," Daisy reminded him.

"Right. I figure we should go down at least once a year and see how he's doing, don't you?"

"Hmm," Daisy murmured, her attention straying to where his fingers were doing the walking over a very sensitive route.

"Well? Are you going to, or aren't you? You still haven't given me a proper answer."

"I was never asked a proper question. Of course, I thoroughly enjoyed the improper ones, but—"

Rolling over, he pressed her down on the pillow and brushed his thumb over her bottom lip again. "Blossom—just say yes and let's get on with it, hmm? We've wasted far too much time as it is."

* * * * *

FOUR UNIQUE SERIES
FOR EVERY WOMAN YOU ARE...

Silhouette Romance®

Tender, delightful, provocative—stories that capture the laughter, the tears, the *joy* of falling in love. Pure romance...straight from the heart!

SILHOUETTE *Desire*®

Go wild with Desire! Passionate, emotional, sensuous stories of fiery romance. With heroines you'll like and heroes you'll *love*, Silhouette Desire never fails to deliver.

Silhouette Special Edition®

Stories of love and life, these powerful novels are tales that you can identify with—romances with "something special" added in! Silhouette Special Edition is entertainment for the heart.

SILHOUETTE·INTIMATE·MOMENTS®

Enter a world where passions run hot and excitement is the rule. Dramatic, larger-than-life and always compelling—Silhouette Intimate Moments will never let you down.

SGENERIC

READERS' COMMENTS ON SILHOUETTE DESIRES

"Thank you for Silhouette Desires. They are the best thing that has happened to the bookshelves in a long time."
—V.W.*, Knoxville, TN

"Silhouette Desires—wonderful, fantastic—the best romance around."
—H.T.*, Margate, N.J.

"As a writer as well as a reader of romantic fiction, I found DESIREs most refreshingly realistic—and definitely as magical as the love captured on their pages."
—C.M.*, Silver Lake, N.Y.

"I just wanted to let you know how very much I enjoy your Silhouette Desire books. I read other romances, and I must say your books rate up at the top of the list."
—C.N.*, Anaheim, CA

"Desires are number one. I especially enjoy the endings because they just don't leave you with a kiss or embrace; they finish the story. Thank you for giving me such reading pleasure."
—M.S.*, Sandford, FL

*names available on request

BE MINE

Daisy Valentine had taken her newly attained look-but-don't-touch attitude south of the border for some sun, surf and *solitude.* Four years as a not-so-gay divorcée had left her wary of any and all relationships—especially those that involved marriageable men!

Professor Gardiner Gentry was on a honeymoon for one, so sharing a dinner table with a hard-as-nails knockout like Daisy didn't exactly soothe his wounded ego. Then why was he suddenly determined to capture this prickly beauty's attention? Had the gentle sea breezes and romantic sunsets of Mexico gone to his head—or had Daisy Valentine taken hold of his heart?

493

1.75
10493

Harlequin Presents...

ELIZABETH GRAHAM

passionate impostor

This
Harlequin
Presents

belongs in the
personal library of

_____